P9-CEG-709

KING
OF SLUGS

A novel by

Michael Frederick

WEST GEORGIA REGIONAL LIBRARY SYSTEM
Neva Lomason Memorial Library

Books by author:

White Shoulders

Places

Ledges

Blue River

The Paper Man

Different

Missouri Madness

Zed

Shy Ann

Drop 50 & Magnify

Summer of '02

Autumn Letters

Stuck

Indie Writer

Dedicated to all slugs.

This book is a work of fiction. Names, characters, places, and incidents are the products of the author's imagination or are used fictitiously. Any resemblance to actual events, locales, or persons, living or dead, is entirely coincidental.

September, 2013/1st printing/2,000 copies
Copyright 2013
all rights reserved

Thanks again, Tony, for your art.
Cover Design by Anthony Conrad

Foreword

THIS NOVEL IS for today's generation of youth looking for hope. For possibilities. For creative interpretations of facts and realities that will lead to the necessary changes this generation of Americans must precipitate in order to become conscious SLUGS—a silly, fictional acronym for Somebody Living Under Great Stress. Since this is a novel, throughout this story I will not capitalize "slugs," for it will be an accepted word to describe most Americans.

Unfortunately, older generations of Americans will not act in unison to change anything. They are overtly entrenched and invested in two political parties that represent big government and the elite of corporate America—massive entities that value votes for tenure and bottom lines for executives and stockholders.

This insanity cannot stand. Slugs must unite. Slugs will decide the future, and this story proves that one person can make a difference. That person can be you!

Adjustments

D ANNY MACK WAS thirty-six in the summer of 1999 when he left his wife and their four-year-old son, Gray, in San Diego. Like most American men, his life changed for the better when his first and only child was born. And like many men, he got married because the girl he was dating got pregnant. Sometimes that kind of "push" into matrimony works out, but most of the time it doesn't. Their divorce papers would be filed while he was on his solitary drive to Omaha, Nebraska, to begin a new life for himself and, eventually, for his son.

Their marriage fell apart because of the incompatibility that financial stress causes. Danny was a struggling telemarketer before he met his future bride. Even though he was good on the phone, he was going from one dead-end job to the next. Yet he learned important things in every call center "boiler room" where he worked. He stayed in this line of work because he was a high school graduate and didn't know what else to do. They lived in San Diego, a place where educated people got the good jobs. Omaha in the 1990s was the perfect place for a guy like Danny; it was the telemarketing capital of the world, and slugs with only a high school diploma could make good money—if they were good on the phone. Danny, the self-proclaimed "King of Slugs," was about to strike gold.

Along that lonely 1,700-mile drive back to the Midwest, he did his best to keep one sustaining thought in his busy mind: *This is for Gray. I am giving him a gift by leaving him now ... so that we can live well together when he's eighteen.*

Danny hailed from Omaha. His parents never married and sent him to Boys Town when he was seven. He left school his junior year at Boys Town and went right to work telemarketing for an extended warranty company in Omaha. Almost immediately his boss took a liking to him and allowed him to live with his family on their farm.

When Danny was a young telemarketer, he dialed and talked slow; cell phones didn't exist. He did everything slow. He walked slow and drove slow. He was slow to get excited and slow to react to things. Danny Mack had a strangeness about him that made other people think he was aloof, separate from them. And yet none of these people ever had the impression that Danny thought he was better than them, even though he'd win every sales contest for whatever product or service he was marketing over the phone.

So the King of Slugs lived at his own pace while the

country graduated to faster and faster ways to communicate. One of his fellow slugs at one of his myriad telemarketing jobs posted on the wall in front of Danny's desk a large newsprint drawing of a snail wearing a crown on its head with the hand-printed inscription below it: "Danny Mack / King of Slugs." It was a few days later after staring at the snail that Danny came up with the acronym for SLUGS as "Somebody Living Under Great Stress."

Danny hated computers; he even gave his Gateway model to Gray before he left San Diego. Fellow slugs would hear from their "king" that technology was too far ahead of human wisdom. Danny often said, "It's not facts or information but the smokescreen of speed that keeps Americans from uniting."

This is the story of Danny and Gray Mack. The father and son are so different in many ways, and yet they have the same incredible goal: to unite America by slowing it down. To reach that goal, Danny Mack had to make the long drive to Omaha and then literally stumble into a telemarketing gold mine along his route in Liberal, Kansas.

Danny's neck and back were killing him from the drive and the emotional stress of his divorce and leaving behind Gray. He only had enough money for gas and to set himself up in a low-rent dive of an apartment in the Omaha area. There was no money to pay a chiropractor to examine and adjust him. But he was the King of Slugs, and his lack of money was not going to stop him from getting the care he needed. Danny had been a chiropractic patient for ten years. "Chiropractic adjustments are my healthcare," he'd tell anyone. "Every three weeks I get adjusted, and I'm able to stay healthy because of them."

He parked his white Ford station wagon and grunted to his feet. The flat, treeless prairie town's business hub was stretched out before him for four blocks of dusty cement and unfamiliar drab storefronts that caused his tired eyes to squint while in search of the relief he knew was somewhere around this section of a town this size.

He gingerly walked into the nearest business, which was a drugstore. "Excuse me," Danny said with a wince to the clerk, "is there a chiropractor nearby who might be taking walk-ins?"

The clerk pointed to his right and said, "There's a chiropractor just two blocks down Main Street on this side of the street."

"Thank you," Danny said with a smile and a brief wave. He left the medicinal smells of the pharmacy with hope that an idea he had developed in Texas would get him an adjustment without spending his diminishing cash.

Most of the way down the sun-blanched sidewalk, Danny purposely kept his mind still, resisting any insidious messages or thoughts about what he would say to this chiropractor. He did the same thing from habit when telemarketing. It was something every chiropractic student learns early: Innate intelligence knows all.

Step after step, moving past the snap-flapping sounds of sun-faded canvas storefront awnings blown by ceaseless Kansas prairie winds, he knew in one micro-flash instant that he, a tired prospector known as the King of Slugs, had discovered gold in a mine above ground that was right there all the time. He was certain that he alone knew about this obvious treasure that was now visible in every passing small business in that dusty Kansas town—an oasis of human commerce that shared its dust and winds and unpredictable weather with the Oklahoma panhandle.

Danny visualized Omaha in his mind, and then he saw clearly that he could excavate this gold mine from Omaha, alone, without looking for some employer who would pay him a substandard wage to market some dead-end product or service that allowed only his ungrateful boss to prosper. Danny Mack then controlled his mind by feeding his brain encouraging self-talk that a prospector like himself needed desperately: *Yes, I'm ready to do this … without a script … and without a dime to spare.*

There it was, the raised-metal lettering on the one-story blond brick building: Liberal Chiropractic. Below that in smaller raised lettering was the name of its proprietor, Dr. James Pratt. Danny pushed open the door, and his six-foot-three-inch frame walked in under the tinkling metal bell that announced his arrival. The air-conditioned room made the sweat on his back feel cooler. A middle-aged receptionist smiled at the stranger with the gray eyes that looked tired from the stress of a long drive. She thought right away the tall man resembled the actor Will Ferrell with his curly brown hair.

Danny stood across from the counter and leaned on it, forcing a courtesy smile and hoping to be filling out the new-patient form attached to the clipboard nearby. "I'm a potential chiropractic patient passing through town … and I'd like to speak with the doctor about getting adjusted."

He stayed at the counter filling out the form because his back was inflamed from driving without taking frequent breaks. The receptionist took his paperwork to the doctor, relaying in his office what Mr. Mack had told her. Within minutes she escorted Danny into the doctor's office, whereupon the stranger was greeted by a friendly middle-aged chiropractor who listened intently to his incredible proposal.

"I'm a ten-year-plus chiropractic patient, Doctor Pratt. I'm on my way to Omaha, Nebraska, from San Diego. I don't have money for an exam and adjustment ... but I do have a creative way to pay you."

The doctor nodded and listened intently.

"I'm a professional telemarketer. If I could use your phone and a phone book, I will call thirty businesses in Liberal, offering all the employees at each business a new-patient special ... like, perhaps, an exam, x-rays if needed, and an adjustment ... all for, say, thirty dollars total. Thirty calls should generate one new patient for you. Maybe more. It should take me about an hour to leave your number and offer with thirty businesses, all with working slugs ... I mean, people who need a good chiropractor."

The doctor finally blinked and asked him, "Do you want to be examined and adjusted before you make the calls ... or after?"

"After. All I need now is a phone and a phone book, a pen, and a little information about you and your hours to schedule appointments." Danny looked up on the wall and saw the doctor's diploma from Palmer Chiropractic School. "I see I'm in good hands. I've been adjusted several times by Palmer graduates," Danny said with a smile.

During that period of calling thirty Liberal businesses for Dr. Pratt, Danny discovered how friendly and open each person was to get the offer. Danny told each prospect, "This offer is good for anyone at your work or for anyone you know, and it's good for as long as you can remember the offer." Danny even scheduled two prospective new patients who wanted to be seen that day. The doctor and receptionist were impressed long after Danny left their office after his exam and adjustment.

On Danny's walk back to his car, he felt better physically because he knew that the innate intelligence of his body had been adjusted back into alignment. Yet it was his marketing for Dr. Pratt that had his spirit feeling as if he'd found a vein of gold. Now he was really anxious to get to Omaha to stake his claim for the new-patient service for chiropractors he decided to name "Telemaster." The beauty of this service was he could call businesses—people who worked during the day—without the pesky residential calling he and every prospector detested.

All the way to Omaha he covered the details of Telemaster in his excited mind, spending hours just figuring how to price his service for the chiropractors he was anxious to call when he got his apartment phone turned on. The way his mind kept bringing in important details he had to know, one right after the other, was amazing to him; yet all the while he kept his car's speed at fifty-five miles per hour and felt certain that some universal law was keeping his speed on the road low because that was the only way he could see all these details that would make Telemaster grow.

Danny had always dreamed of finding something like this, a product or service that he could turn into gold for his slugs that he would train his way. *Is this how something feels when something truly good comes to you?* he asked himself as more and more important little things came to him. Like how the pace of Telemaster slugs had to be slow in order to create a relaxed environment, the same state he would reach when he meditated before work and during every break he took, while other slugs in dead-end jobs chain-smoked and were the same talking heads outside of work as they were on the phone.

The rest of Danny's drive was filled with the new adjustments he would make at Telemaster. It was as if the fun had already begun. No more guilty thoughts about leaving Gray and a marriage that was way beyond bad. The oppressive fear of his lack of money vanished, along with all the lousy jobs that used to haunt him and flinch his restive body awake when sleeping. They were replaced by his slow, thudding pulse of acute awareness that he never wanted to lose.

Did Doctor Pratt's adjustment in Liberal cause this? Danny asked himself. *If so, it will go away in time. Or have I found paradise on earth with this new service? It will be so easy to start and hand off to other slugs who will love the working environment I know how to create and sustain.*

Training for Slugs

D ANNY SIGNED A lease on a studio apartment in Council Bluffs, Iowa, just across the Missouri River from Omaha. Right away he activated an unlimited long-distance phone service in his furnished studio and called from his kitchen counter on a barstool. Gray's billfold-sized picture stood against the wall on the counter so that he could see his motivation. Danny would wait until the weekend to call Gray, not wanting to disturb his son's school routine during the week. Besides, he wanted to have more Telemaster progress behind him.

He used his phone to find a used but free 1998 Omaha metro crisscross phone directory from a Council Bluffs collection agency. The directory listed every business by zip code in the entire area. He then was able to pound purposefully his push-button desk phone while wearing his headset and calling chiropractors all over Omaha. With each contact he left his concise, professional message with the receptionist about his "new-patient telemarketing service to businesses," emphasizing *businesses,* while his relaxed gray eyes remained on Gray's photo.

Six chiropractors returned Danny's call the first day wanting information about his service. His goal was a simple one: For $300.00 and fifteen hours of telemarketing to businesses only, the practice should get a minimum of four new scheduled patients. A special would be offered to area businesses solicited that allowed each employee who came in as a new patient to have an exam, x-rays (if needed), and an adjustment—all for just $30.00.

Since Danny had no references except Dr. Pratt in Liberal, he diminished his prospective chiropractors' skepticism by setting an appointment to meet with each doctor at their office. At that meeting he would get all the scheduling information he needed and go over his typed phone script. He would also show each doctor his homemade three-by-five appointment/lead slip and the businesses in his zip code calling area in the directory. In almost every instance, Danny would leave the doctor's office with his three hundred dollar check made out to Telemaster. Then he would head for his next appointment in another exclusive zip code.

Within the first two weeks, the King of Slugs was calling for six doctors in Omaha and one in Council Bluffs. From eight in the morning until five at night, he pounded businesses with his slow, deliberate pitch to whomever answered the phone and kept a detailed log of each call's result. He was scheduling a solid appointment every hour on the average, then moving to the next doctor. He did his best to ensure every doctor got a scheduled new patient from him.

It didn't take long for the doctors on Danny's service to know they had made a good marketing decision. They all knew that three hundred dollars was not much to invest, compared to other marketing services that might guarantee patients but charge thousands of dollars plus start-up fees.

Danny put a value of $20.00 an hour on his service because of his low overhead. It was a good value for new doctors to try his service, and it bolstered his desire to hire slugs as fast as possible. He knew from his appointment-setting experience for another health-related service that he would average one appointment per hour, and half of his appointments would show. But he also knew from experience that other slugs he trained would average an appointment every two hours and half of those would show. That's how he felt confident telling his doctors that for their $300.00 investment, they should get four patients for fifteen hours' worth of calling.

After the first three weeks, all of the doctors subscribing to his service renewed. Danny was ready to grow. Each weekend he walked around Council Bluffs to look at available office space close to his apartment. He found the perfect place that was eight hundred square feet and already furnished with a telemarketing set-up: chairs and wall-mounted desks with dividers, plus a dozen phone lines already installed. It was a timeshare boiler room that went belly up and skipped out of its one-year lease.

Danny signed a one-year lease at $450.00 a month plus

heat and water, and he paid a $300.00 damage deposit. As a bonus, Danny got to use all the furnishings. He was ready to run an ad in the *Council Bluffs News* and build the empire he knew he could.

Gray got a call every Saturday and Sunday from his dad. Danny would tell his five-year-old son every detail about Telemaster, and his bright boy would understand everything.

"Gray, what's your favorite color that makes you feel happy?"

"I like blue like the sky … and green like trees," the boy answered into his headset that his dad taught him to use whenever he called.

"You know what my favorite color is?" Danny asked.

"Yes!"

"What is it?"

"Gray!" the boy laughed.

"Right! So that's blue and green for you and gray for me. Those are the three colors I'm going to have on the walls of my new office after one year. I can show you the office and colors when you visit me next summer. How does that sound?"

"Good!"

"Okay, we've been talking for thirty minutes. What do we do now?"

"Change ears!" Gray blared.

"Right!"

Both of them switched around their microphones so they could put the cushioned earpiece over the other ear.

"Did you switch ears?' Danny asked.

"Yes!"

"You know why we switch ears?"

"So my brain is good and my neck doesn't hurt."

"Very good, Gray! And have you been using my computer I gave you?"

"Yes!" The boy looked over on his little desk at the Gateway screen with the video game Donkey Kong displayed.

When their call ended, Gray removed his headset, sat down on his little chair in front of his computer, and moved his mouse to a search engine before typing on his keyboard "cheats for donkey kong."

*　　*　　*

Shelly and Burt Rand were a young married couple looking for part-time work while going to school. Shelly was in her final year of her business degree while Burt already had his business degree and was on track to be a CPA within a year. They were the first part-time slugs Danny hired, each one working the same four-hour shift, 9:00 a.m. to 1:00 p.m., Monday through Friday.

The Rands liked Danny instantly, especially his way of running a telemarketing business with a ten-minute break after each hour of calling. Danny's slugs had bottled water and fresh ozone in the windowless office space. Slugs wore quality headsets with long cords so that standing and moving around while talking on the phone was possible. At the beginning of each shift, all slugs would assemble for a short "pep rally" which included a laughing session. They would laugh together openly and out loud, which helped set the mood for a relaxed, positive, enjoyable shift.

Since Telemaster had only one directory, Danny used a box cutter to remove the pages and highlight the zip codes. Pencils were used instead of pens so the previous calls could be erased if they ran out of marking space for each call. Each chiropractic office had its own manila folder that held the calling pages and personalized phone script with all necessary information needed.

The King of Slugs used the phone at a workstation between Shelly and Burt. He trained his slugs his way, using his relaxed pace and voice, and showing them first-hand the myriad little nuances that made each call "as easy as possible for you and for all the slugs you call."

It took a few days until his new slugs got used to the new marketing concept. "We are here to create teamwork energy that is positive and contagious versus the competitive, stressful way American slugs are trained to be number one and then compensated with bonuses and commissions." He would remind his growing number of slugs, "That's a formula for negative energy, burnout, and weak appointments."

Within a month at the Telemaster location in Council Bluffs, all seven chiropractors were renewing their marketing plans every two weeks. In addition, they had examined and adjusted every slug that called for them free of charge. Thanks to good references, Danny was well on his way to filling all twenty-four seats for both shifts.

Danny raised his price of his service to $350.00, which included a $50.00 directory fee so that doctors helped pay for his growing shelf of directories and phone books from smaller towns. After three months Telemaster was maxed-out and keeping sixty doctors happy with the new-patient service while generating over twenty thousand dollars a month in revenue. And the list of chiropractors waiting to subscribe to Telemaster's marketing services was growing.

Telemaster's slugs were happy getting paid ten dollars an hour with no commission in a fun, positive environment. Other part-time telemarketing slugs in the Omaha area were calling the upstart Telemaster; however, since turnover was low, the waiting list was growing with slugs wanting to work for Danny. That was another way Danny knew his service was working; he didn't have to run any employment ads. Yet not just any slug could work for Danny Mack. Every slug at Telemaster was either treating with a chiropractor or had in the past. They could not just work there because they had telemarketing experience. Each slug had to be pro-chiropractic or they couldn't call for the King of Slugs.

Danny could see that he was ready to grow into a bigger location with CPA Burt Rand now handling Telemaster's books and taxes. His wife Shelly answered all incoming calls while calling for new patients during both shifts. Shelly was happy to quit school knowing she was in on the ground floor of a growing company with huge potential.

Eight months into his lease, Danny found the perfect new location in an old warehouse building in the Omaha Rail and Commerce Historic District of Old Market in downtown Omaha. The eight-story building had the potential for unlimited growth and the flexibility he needed to grow into it. He signed a two-year lease for $2,200.00 a month to lease the massive first floor with first option on other floors until the lease was up.

Danny had Shelly and Burt run the Council Bluffs location while he got the new location going. He also moved out of his dive studio apartment in Council Bluffs and into a nice one-bedroom loft apartment in Old Market that was only six blocks from his new Telemaster location.

*   *   *

A few short months before Danny moved into his new location, Gray was eagerly anticipating his first summer vacation with his dad since the divorce. Gray was interested in how things worked, and not just when it came to cheating at Donkey Kong. One night Gray's mother came into her son's room to make sure he was asleep. Instead, she found him under his covers with a flashlight peering inside his computer's modem after removing its cover with a screwdriver. Yes, Gray Mack was a precocious little boy who liked to find out how things worked. Unlike his dad, Gray was into anything technical, especially the latest gadgets he'd see at the mall.

Gray Summers

SUMMERTIME WAS DANNY and Gray's favorite time of every year, even before they were separated by divorce. That first summer after the divorce, Danny drove to San Diego in a leased new gray Camry and picked up his five-year-old boy at his house. Gray's mom gave Danny a hug then kissed her son goodbye for six weeks. Although it made her heartsick to see Gray leave, she was happy to see her only child so excited to be going on summer vacation with his dad.

Gray wouldn't remember most of the places they would see every summer, but he always recalled the fun of just being together. Like any conscious parent, Danny did his best to let his son feel that he was loved by his father.

At five years old, Gray was at the age where he wanted to know important things about his parents. He asked questions and listened to the words that made the empty spaces reserved for all knowledge of his father's life in his boy's mind start to fill up with images and stories that would stay with him a lifetime. And his father was aware of this when he answered his son's question about his own parents—why they sent him to Boys Town and never came back for him.

"Well … my parents just knew they could never take care of me like your mom and I take care of you. So they put me in a place for boys who needed a good place to live until they could live on their own."

"Mom said you were poor and lived in your car for a long time after you left that place."

"Yeah, I did. I'll always remember that time, and it makes me appreciate what I have today."

"Wasn't it crowded in your car?"

"Yes, it was," Danny laughed, "and I never want to go back to living that way again."

Gray would always recall the Mexican chiropractor they visited in El Centro, California, off I-8 on their way to the Grand Canyon. Danny told Gray that he called this doctor from Omaha and told him he'd stop in to get a complimentary adjustment on his drive back to Omaha.

"I gave him some references, and he told me I was smart because I could write off my vacation this way. I said, 'I know … you're the fourth chiropractor I'll see on my trip.'"

Gray was confused, but the way his dad laughed when he told the story made Gray laugh.

The doctor in El Centro even adjusted Gray for free, since Gray had been adjusted by a chiropractor a few times every year since he was a baby. The man was a Mexican doctor and spoke English very well. Gray recalled the doctor wanting to try his dad's service and said he wanted to be put on his waiting list. After they left the doctor's office, they walked to a nearby Mexican restaurant that the doctor said had good food.

From there they went to Yuma, their first stop in Arizona. They toured the Yuma Territorial Prison and stopped to visit with another chiropractor, a woman who was anxious to try Danny's service because she was new to the area.

Even the panoramic stop at the Grand Canyon couldn't compete with the thrill Danny was anticipating in Omaha when showing Gray what he'd accomplished there. He had left Omaha on vacation when he was up to his ears getting the new location ready for his two dozen Council Bluffs slugs still working there, even though he had managed to transition in another two dozen slugs working both shifts at the new location that he named "Slug Central." He had moved experienced slugs from Council Bluffs to Slug Central to train new slugs, while there was a slow-moving trail of new slugs filling the empty seats in Council Bluffs who were also being trained by experienced slugs.

Slug Central was being constructed over eight weeks by a licensed and bonded Mexican-American construction crew based out of Omaha. The Telemaster boss had left during a cacophony of electric saws and drills, hammers, and painters with drop cloths and ladders working around his slugs. Blue-enriched white lighting to reduce eye strain was being installed when Danny left. Recycled wood was painted blue, green, and gray on the cubicle dividers that held two workstations in each cube, plenty of space for two slugs to call with their backs to each other. Danny wanted one experienced slug in the same cube with a new slug in training.

It was in a Grand Canyon gift shop that Danny bought Gray a video camera with a tripod so they had memories of their first summer vacation together. Danny was surprised how much Gray loved using the camera, not to mention the creative flair he had for filming obscure things. His dad thought he was incredibly mature for a five-year-old. Gray's camera captured so many details of their trip: the swirling straw in the wind outside a Texas Dairy Queen; the steady scene of a homeless man curled up into a ball behind a dumpster at a truck stop; a hundred comical scenes of his dad goofing off at gas pumps, pretending to be blind and unable to find the gas tank; the time when they were in a restaurant and Danny covered his eyes with spoons and then was unable to find his straw inside his milkshake. There was plenty of film of the two of them jumping together on motel beds, as well as one long stretch of a dark room at the Ghost Rider Motel where they filmed while they were sleeping because they wanted to see if they could capture footage of any ghosts that might appear.

They arrived in Omaha with a new video playback machine to watch their vacation in Danny's loft apartment. Gray had his first Audio Player with ear buds, along with a stack of CDs they picked out together and sang along to the music from San Diego all the way to Omaha. They started reliving their travel adventure in the early evening and watched their vacation video all night, laughing at all the things they filmed during their four-day drive to Omaha.

The next morning father and son walked hand-in-hand the six blocks to the new Telemaster location, where Gray got the royal tour by the boss. Danny introduced his boy to each of the slugs working that shift. Gray was impressed by the way these people who worked for his dad really liked his dad, and he was instantly taken aback by how their favorite colors were painted on his dad's walls and cubicle dividers.

Danny was satisfied with the construction progress and the appointment set-and-show ratios at both locations while he was away. Shelly provided him the figures from her computer desk in the middle of Slug Central next to where Danny's office would be located by the end of the remodeling.

Danny and Gray spent the next five weeks vacationing in Omaha. They toured museums, went to restaurants and movies, and listened to music. All of it was done around the big transition when Telemaster in Council Bluffs was moved to Slug Central, and all the remodeling was done around the working slugs.

When the Telemaster remodeling was finished at Slug Central, it had a cubicle capacity for five hundred slugs. During this five-week period, Danny personally called from a small desk in the middle of Slug Central, training another slug to secure doctors on their new-patient service. All the while Gray sat patiently in a chair close to his dad, or Shelly would let him play a video game on her computer at her desk twenty feet from Danny's desk.

Now Shelly and Burt were working together, each one working fifty hours a week trying to get and keep the Telemaster business running as smoothly as possible. "I don't know if I could do this without them," Danny confessed to Gray one day when they were walking to lunch.

Gray was not like most boys at his age. He was interested in every little detail about his father's growing business, and he even came up with a few ideas of his own. This was due to the fact that his dad encouraged creativity and despised competition, telling his son, "Don't be afraid to fail and try new things. Telemaster works because I saw what doesn't work. Determination and creative attitudes win. Everyone wins if we don't try to beat the next guy down."

Gray even came up with a great idea: having a daycare at Telemaster so kids could play there while their mom or dad worked.

Summer after summer Danny was amazed at how tech-smart his son was. He showed more and more loner tendencies that concerned Gray's mother more than it did his father. One summer vacation in Omaha when Gray was twelve, he set up a webcam on his father's computer screen at home and at work. That way father and son could Skype, having face-to-face video calls when Gray was home in San Diego.

Usually every day they would Skype three or four times a day—usually right after school, after homework, and then before bed. It was important to Danny that he wasn't just a weekend chat-on-the-phone absentee dad.

What they most liked to talk about was Telemaster and all the details involved with a growing business concern. By the time Gray was to turn eighteen, the summer before his senior year, Gray knew more about Telemaster than his father did. Except for the phone sales and prospecting, Gray Mack oversaw and created every technical aspect that brought in state-of-the-art business communications. It was common knowledge at Telemaster that Gray was the young genius who kept the company's phones and computers going. "Thanks to Gray we came out of the Stone Age," Shelly and Burt often said.

Each summer Gray would improve the company's ability to communicate. No more cumbersome phone books and page sorting with files everywhere. Manual phone dialing was history, and so were wasteful gaps of silence because of delayed connections. Every slug had a computer with organized lists making fast connections, which saved the company a fortune in productivity and time management.

It had been Danny's idea to get Gray involved with smart phones, iPads, and anything else that would enable him to communicate with his son about the business whenever they were separated. Being tech savvy wasn't something his father had to force or coerce Gray into; Danny just supplied him with the latest tools and knew that it would also somehow help his only child get along in a technical world his father knew nothing about.

Gray lost interest in video games when he was about eight, especially the violent ones he called "gun rats." He was more passive and creative like his dad, preferring to take photographs and digital images of places and things he found interesting. One time when Gray was only nine years old, he sent his dad time-elapsed images of scudding clouds in San Diego that showed incredible changes in light. The images were mixed in with music he selected. Danny had always been impressed with his son's creativity and maturity.

Father and Son

B Y THE SUMMER of 2012, Gray was living with his dad in a two-bedroom loft in the same apartment building. For twelve years Gray had looked forward to his senior year at Midtown High in Omaha. After over a decade of daily video contact, it hardly seemed to Gray or his dad that they had lived apart for most of the last twelve years. The best thing about this father-and-son relationship was that they enjoyed each other without the egotistical game of dominance and submission.

Danny had zero interest in learning about technology, but Gray wanted to learn how his father was able to slow down his life while the rest of the country seemed to be speeding up. Every little quirk or nuance about his dad Gray would observe and file away without comment or judgment.

The King of Slugs had rituals he would perform every day of his life. He had his morning meditation on an inversion table where he hung upside down, he would drink only alkaline water, and he was always looking for ways to making the working environment better for his slugs.

His slugs didn't just appreciate Danny, they loved him. He trained them all to slow down and experience life in a relaxed state. Compared to most boiler rooms and considering that most slugs were chain-smoking lost souls, Danny was their beloved king. He taught them how to stay healthy in a world gone mad with alcohol, nicotine, and other drug abuse.

He knew as a father that he could lose Gray to some think-tank company in California if he didn't teach him how to love the company they both had built. Gray even said he'd skip his senior year to join some company who could use his skills. But he really didn't want to. It had taken Danny just ten years, with Gray's help, to have over three thousand slugs working for Telemaster on all eight floors of the building Danny had bought five years previous.

Since the time Gray was twelve, Burt and Shelly and even Danny had consulted Gray nearly every day about some technical problem they were having with computers, the phone system, software designed for Telemaster, something Danny wanted changed or added to the Telemaster website, or Danny's newsletter for slug members called *Peaceful Trails*.

Gray learned over time that early in his father's

telemarketing career his father became conscious of the stress that the competitive push to be number one in America's culture was causing the people who were trapped in that game. To stop that insanity Danny began living his mantra: Slow down … there's plenty of time. He would say it to his mind while dialing a phone number, while waiting for his prospect to answer, and a thousand more times a day. Danny knew other slugs were consumed with stressful thoughts like, *Gotta get this one. … Keep getting 'em sold. … Dial another number quick. … Gotta get more calls in. … Need one more. … More, more, more! … It's a numbers game.*

For Gray it was amazing to watch his dad, the self-named King of Slugs. He learned that every place his dad had worked, other slugs would see his slow and deliberate dialing. Then they'd hear his lazy, relaxed words so casual and laid back that any slug who worked close to him automatically started slowing down, talking slower, relaxing more and more. Danny Mack always had the most leads, sales or appointments, and he won every contest without ever raising his voice or his blood pressure.

During the first summer Gray lived in Omaha, before starting his final year of high school, he could see clearly that his father was a natural leader for slugs. And he did it all with his eyes closed—another relaxing technique for his eyes that he had learned from an old pro slug in a boiler room. The man had glaucoma and needed to reduce the strain from reading small print and phone numbers on lists in his cramped, windowless cubicle. It was a dead-end scenario that would drive other less creative slugs to liquor stores and bar stools before heading home after every shift.

This snail's pace that Danny Mack was known for had been shared with thousands of his Telemaster slugs, as well as other slugs that subscribed to his popular newsletter, *Peaceful Trails*. It had all been done with the help of Gray, who had built, updated and maintained his father's website and newsletter since he was in the seventh grade.

Gray, besides having his father's six-foot-three-inch height, also inherited his "slowness" in every way except when it came to tech support. It drove his mother crazy seeing her son cloned not only with her ex-husband's physical likeness, but also his slow mannerisms that never failed to clash with her lively personality.

Conscious Telemaster

TELEMASTER WAS MORE than a good place to work in Omaha. It had a reputation among experienced slugs as being so employee friendly that it made other businesses seem like prisons by comparison.

By the late fall of 2012, Telemaster was located in two buildings that were connected to each other by a fourth-floor skywalk. The seven-story building next to Slug Central had once been the home office and warehouse for the Butter Roast Coffee Company. Danny converted the lower four floors to four hundred slug stations for eight hundred phones. The top three floors were converted to 110 furnished studio apartments. Forty similar apartments were located on the top two floors of the Slug Central building. These compact apartments were rented out to 110 previously homeless single men and women, who now made up nearly three percent of Telemaster's employees. Also, many of these resident slugs were getting drug or alcohol abuse counseling. There was no alcohol or any drug use permitted—including smoking—by any of the residents. Danny wanted only healthy slugs working for him, and very few slugs who smoked ever did so during working hours. If resident slugs broke any rules, they were evicted from their apartments and terminated from working at Telemaster. Danny was tough but fair.

Burt, the company CPA, created an equitable formula so that these resident slugs paid twenty percent of their twenty-hour-per week wages toward their rent, which included utilities. Since these were the tenuous slugs with addictions, the rent payments were deducted from their paychecks every two weeks. Only twenty-five percent of the tenants were booted out consistently, which was pretty good—all things considered.

No children under eighteen were permitted to live in the apartments. For liability reasons Danny had to go along with that stipulation in order to keep from raising the rent. These once-forgotten lost souls, if they stayed sober for ninety days, were getting free healthcare, living with a roof over their heads, and earning a living wage. They truly loved their King of Slugs. Even the ones who had to be terminated.

Since Danny had been homeless and living in his car in his youth, he wanted to make sure he did something for other unfortunate souls who needed a break. He wanted to help anyone with ambition get a good job and a roof over their head. So he trained these lost souls and gave them an apartment that would be prorated against their wages, as well as any food they charged against their earnings in Telemaster's health-conscious café and coffeehouse. No vending machines were allowed. There was even a fully-equipped workout room with treadmills, stair-climbers and other modern exercise equipment. Alcohol consumption and other drug use or tobacco use was not permitted in the Telemaster buildings; and no healthcare plans were offered to any slugs who were addicted to alcohol, tobacco, or any other drugs. Usually, homeless slugs willing to be trained to work for Telemaster were given a ninety-day probationary period to prove—mostly to themselves—that they could change their lives by changing their lifestyles. Addicts who needed professional help to get clean and sober were given all the state and federal resource information available and offered a job once they were successful.

Danny Mack wanted to create a work environment that made sense. He had learned the hard way in dozens of boiler rooms what not to do. Chiropractic clients in the area would be scheduled into Telemaster to adjust the constant flow of new slugs calling for them in modern treatment rooms furnished by Telemaster.

All these amenities were only a small part of why Telemaster slugs loved their king. They knew Danny didn't have to provide anything more than a boiler room with phones, desks, chairs, phone books, two toilets, and maybe a vending machine. And he certainly didn't have to provide any benefits.

Danny was well aware that if he withheld, he could

never prosper. Since Danny had worked on the dark side of telemarketing, he believed early on that if he could create the right service—like Telemaster—he would train and treat his slugs with the respect they deserved. He would provide a working environment that promoted relaxation and cooperation versus stress and competition.

Upon entering the front door of Telemaster on the raised cement platform that skirted three sides of both buildings, Marv Lewis, an elderly retired cop, was there to greet everyone who entered. Marv wore many hats for Telemaster. He was the resident manager of the Butter Roast Apartments, as well as the custodian superintendent and head security guard who opened and closed Telemaster. Resident slugs had pointed out to them in their lease agreement that Marv could enter and inspect any apartment without notice.

At the start of every shift, Marv's warm smile blessed every slug who entered the peaceful workplace. Metaphysical "Soundscape" music played throughout the massive Slug Central. Upon entering the building, the first thing anyone would see was a bronze-colored giant Styrofoam snail suspended from the ceiling of the massive room that turned slowly 360 degrees. Above the snail was the Telemaster company motto: "Slow down ... there's plenty of time."

Every slug at Telemaster at one time or another remarked how they would arrive at work after driving through the busy Omaha metro traffic, and immediately upon hearing the relaxing music and seeing that happy snail would begin to relax. Coming to work was easy because they were in a space of order and teamwork in a world that cared about them.

Cluster Flocks and Immigration

GRAY'S FIRST WEEK of being a senior at Midtown High, he played a part in a typical King of Slugs way of resolving problems. There was about thirty minutes left in his last class of the day, study hall. Gray liked his class schedule because it gave him an hour to get any homework done so the rest of the day was his. It was an Indian summer afternoon that reminded Gray of when his dad would take him to the Omaha zoo every summer.

Gray's miniature wireless earpiece started to vibrate inside his right eardrum in Study Hall. He knew it was his dad calling and that it must be important, likely something related to work. Discreetly, he answered his cell phone by palming it close to his mouth. His dad's words couldn't have been more relaxed, considering he was calling from his moving car on I-80 between Lincoln and Omaha. He was headed east to pick Gray up at school after getting three new Lincoln doctors on his service. His dad had witnessed four semi-trailer trucks from the same company "cluster flocking" traffic by blocking both lanes and impeding vehicles from passing them. It was an illegal—not to mention irritating and dangerous—game to play when traveling. Danny was content traveling sixty miles per hour in the seventy-five-mile-per-hour zone because he knew he was saving fuel and, of course, he was in no hurry. However, he could see up ahead that the growing number of vehicles trying to pass these four pinheads was somehow pleasing to their little brains, despite the fact that it was causing stress to several travelers for several miles. That's when Danny called his son in study hall and said calmly, "Get me the phone number of Deck Transfer in Des Moines."

Right away Gray found the number on his smart phone and discreetly gave it to his dad.

"Thanks. See ya soon. Bye."

Danny quickly dialed the number Gray gave him. The dispatcher answered, "Deck Transfer, this is Jim. May I help you?"

"Jim?"

"Yes, sir."

"This is Danny Mack from Telemaster of Omaha."

"Yes, sir."

"I'm driving east on I-80, just past mile marker

forty-seven, and four of your drivers are intentionally blocking traffic, preventing anyone from passing in the left lane. I have a lot of professional associates, Jim, that ship with your company. Do you know how much business my associates do with your company annually, Jim?"

After an awkward pause Danny continued: "Will you please call those four idiots right now and tell 'em they're going to be costing you big business?"

"Can you see any of the truck numbers, sir?"

"No, I can't. And it's too dangerous to get close enough to look. I'll give those pinheads thirty seconds before I start calling my fellow business owners."

"Yes, sir."

Danny closed his cell phone and watched the impish cluster-flocking still going on up ahead with several cars tailgating in the blocked passing lane. Less than a minute later, Danny watched the two truckers who were blocking the passing lane speed up and move into the right lane, allowing the blocked traffic to pass. Danny smiled down at the cell phone in his hand, knowing how so many problems in this world could be resolved at the speed of sound with a simple phone call.

*   *   *

One afternoon after school, Shelly dropped a curt note onto Danny's desk that read, "Roberto/San Antonio." Danny got up from his desk, walked over to Gray seated at his computer station, and placed the note beside his keyboard. Right away Gray accessed the Telemaster employee files, and instantly the smiling face of Roberto Carlos Perez appeared on the screen. Gray read the profile on the slug to his father. "Age twenty-nine. Married to Isabella, age twenty-six. U.S. citizens with two children, a boy and a girl ages two and three ... both here in daycare."

"Does Isabella work?" his boss asked.

"Uh ... yes. She's a housekeeper at the Worldwide Inn in downtown Omaha."

"That place is new, so she hasn't been there long."

"Right. And they live in an apartment in Omaha," Gray added.

Gray followed his dad out of the office and into a stairway. On the main doors of each floor were listed the cities of the client markets served by the slugs on that floor. The second floor's doors were labeled "Atlanta, Albuquerque, Austin, Phoenix, Tucson." They climbed past the third floor to the fourth which was labeled, "San Antonio, Dallas/Ft. Worth, Houston." Down the fourth floor hallway they walked as the song "We're Going To Be Friends" by the White Stripes played softly from the sound system that Gray had designed and installed. They came to an open office door marked "San Antonio" and entered the partitioned room with four cubes that faced north toward the large window looking out over the Omaha skyline. There were four Hispanic-American slugs calling from their workstations, three females and Roberto. Danny waited until Roberto was finished with his call to a Spanish-speaking prospect.

Roberto removed his headset, spun around in his chair, and stood up to greet his boss in perfect English with a handshake. "Hello, Mr. Danny."

"Please sit, Roberto. This is Gray, my son."

Gray and Roberto exchanged friendly nods, and Danny told Roberto that he heard from Personnel that he has a problem. "What is it?" Danny asked his slug.

"My wife was fired today from her job because she doesn't speak English as well as they want her to."

"But they knew that when they hired her, didn't they?" Danny was confused.

"Yes, but they said she has to take a class and get better. We practice at home every night … but she's not learning it fast enough for them," Roberto explained.

"I see. … Where is she now?"

"She's on her way to a bus stop to go home."

"Does she have a cell phone?"

"Yes, she does."

"Call Isabella right now and tell her she can work in the daycare here until we can help her find another job. And she can learn English here with your kids in the daycare."

"Thank you so much, Mr. Danny," Roberto said while vigorously shaking his boss's hand. "I'll call her right away."

"Have her go to the daycare when she gets here."

"Yes, thank you." Roberto was excited and donned his headset and called his wife.

They left "San Antonio" and headed for the daycare on the main floor of Slug Central near the exercise room. On the way Gray followed his dad into the New Client room where the most experienced slugs rotated to once every two months for a week of calling new doctors for their service. When Danny entered the room of eight cubes, he got right to the point with the first slug who was free to talk.

"Isabella Perez needs a job as a housekeeper in a downtown Omaha hotel. Find her some leads to apply for work, and give the leads to her later this afternoon in the daycare."

"Got it," the slug wrote down the information and Danny left the room.

In the brightly colored daycare, over a hundred preschool-aged kids were playing. Danny went over to his daycare director and said, "Isabella Perez has two kids here. When she gets here, give her some work to do and have her sit in on an English lesson with the kids."

The director smiled and Danny exited the room. Gray had watched the scene from the doorway, impressed with the way his dad handled a problem for one of his slugs. For the first time since moving to Omaha, Gray was certain this was the kind of good work he wanted to do.

Early Release

BEFORE 10:42 A.M. on December 17, 2012, Telemaster was the largest outbound telemarketing service in America. But at 10:43 a.m. three thousand slugs in Slug Central sat in front of blank computer screens because every phone was shut down. Telemaster, for the time being, was out of business. The six shift managers were at different workstations addressing the problem until exasperated. Ten minutes later, all six floor managers converged on the main floor with one voicing their united opinion, "We'd better go tell the boss that all the phones are down."

"Call him on your cell phone," another manager suggested.

"He won't answer his phone now," another manager said as she looked at her wristwatch. "This is his quiet time."

They headed toward the center of Slug Central as three thousand slugs stood and stretched in their cubes.

The shift managers knew they had to go through Shelly, who was seated behind her desk in front of Danny's office door. They could all see inside Danny's nine-hundred-square-foot office because its four walls were a mint-green glass ten feet high with no ceiling of its own. Behind the glass they could see lush trees and plants growing in Nebraska soil. There were tufts of blue-eyed grass mixed with wild yellow prairie buttercups, and the red-pink prairie rose was potted in a dozen places. Shelly was thirty-four years old, five-feet-two-inches tall, and thought of by everyone who worked there as Danny's sister. The two fought openly and often, but got over it quickly and worked in tandem to keep the company flourishing.

"All the phones are down," one manager informed Danny's personal secretary.

"In both buildings?" she asked with incredulity, looking over the top of the pink-framed glasses planted on the end of her tiny nose.

Six nodding heads compelled her to get up at once and enter the office door behind her.

The relaxing new-age song that her boss always meditated to, "Veracruz" by Nicholas Gunn, was playing inside the office. She stepped over to the CD player and turned it off.

In the far corner, facing east and meditating Indian fashion on a Persian rug between two thick-leaved olive trees, sat Telemaster's King of Slugs. He opened his relaxed gray eyes as Shelly's quick footsteps sounded urgent, approaching then stopping in front of him.

"All the phones are shut down. You better call Gray."

He scratched his curly brown hair, got up, walked calmly to his desk, and speed-dialed a number on his cell phone.

Gray was in Algebra class when his phone vibrated inside his earpiece. This was why he sat in the last row at the back of the class. He answered discreetly with a breath exhalation.

"The phones are all down."

Gray closed his phone and retrieved his backpack as the teacher's chalk moved across the blackboard. He opened his laptop and logged into Telemaster's software for the phone system that he had designed. He typed in a code, analyzed what he saw, and did some discreet troubleshooting.

Meanwhile, thousands of faces on the other side of the mint-green glass were waiting and watching as their leader sat at Gray's computer station waiting for his son's call. Danny held his cell phone in one hand, staying as calm as possible considering he had three thousand slugs making ten to fifteen dollars an hour for doing nothing.

Seconds seemed like hours when he was aware of the crowd watching his every move. Then "Gray" lit up on his ringing cell phone.

"Dad," he whispered.

"Yeah?"

"See the blue button to the left on the middle panel?"

"Yeah."

"Push it in and hold it for three seconds."

"Okay." He did what his son told him to.

"See that red button on the lower panel?"

"Yeah."

"Don't touch it. Sorry … just messin' with ya. You should be good to go."

"Really? That's it?"

"Gotta go."

"Thanks," Danny said too late for Gray to hear him.

Danny came out of his office. The chatter stopped as he walked to the nearest workstation, donned a headset, heard a dial tone, and smiled. Then from inside the cube he spread his arms out wide and yelled "WE'RE BACK IN BUSINESS!" As his slugs hustled back to their workstations, Danny looked up to the giant snail hanging from the ceiling in the middle of his massive Slug Central and smiled.

Walking back to his office, Danny Mack's body language had returned to the animated cheerleader he was most every day. His six shift managers were waiting by Shelly's desk for any instructions.

"We were down for only sixteen minutes!" the boss exclaimed. "Let them know we can't make up for lost time … but we *can* enjoy the time we have and set more appointments with a positive attitude."

With those sage words of advice, his managers took off in six directions anxious to return to the work they loved—and for the man who led by example.

His loyal slugs would work as a team without competition. If one slug calling for a doctor in one city was having trouble setting appointments, that particular slug would post a "Slug Alert" on his or her computer screen. Other slugs who were ahead of pace and looking good on their appointment-setting would make calls for the trailing slug from the list of prospects in that particular calling area. It was another feature and benefit Gray Mack created in order to help his dad's business succeed in the twenty-first century.

Danny was aware that he could have called his Omaha phone service representative; but if the rep was busy and couldn't get to Telemaster right away, the down time would have cost Danny thousands of dollars and several hours. He might possibly have had to send three thousand slugs home with lost pay, in addition to having doctors wondering what happened. But all it cost him was sixteen minutes. *We can make up some lost energy,* he told himself.

And they did. At times like this Danny liked to show what teamwork and cooperation could do compared to the American notion: "There's number one—and the rest are losers."

Danny had trained all twelve of his shift managers for this "all hands on deck" mode that now he watched unfold before his eyes. He walked with such poise and confidence that his body language stirred a desire in every slug on that shift to make up for any lost appointments before the next shift started. Going from cube to cube on every floor in both buildings, his words were fueling creative energy that was contagious.

Danny knew that if he could coach over fifty percent of his slugs to truly work together as a team, they would prove to any negative slugs that they were wasting energy. And as the negative attitudes turned positive, these individuals would begin to move out of their fear-based minds and into a growing wave of positive energy that would work together like one united family.

"Stay with your *slow* delivery, slugs! Imagine that your prospect is waiting for your call. Get an appointment and move to a screen that needs an appointment. Help all your brothers and sisters get what they want. Let your prospect hear your sweetest and happiest voice. Take your time and *breathe*. Relax those neck muscles when you're talking. And remember: This is *not* a competition! Stay with the feeling of wanting to help others, and good things will happen."

As he walked along the clear cubes exhorting these positive words of encouragement, he could see and feel that most of his slugs were holding onto hope by using the positive energy needed to reach any goal without stress or the awful fear promoted in American culture of "being wrong" and losing out to competition.

"Stay relaxed!" he encouraged them as his favorite song for meditating, "Veracruz," began playing throughout the massive calling center.

Danny stopped to listen to his song while leaning his chin on one of his clear cubes. He closed his eyes and imagined seeing his slugs acting in concert as one body of united energy. This was Danny's kind of patriotism—not some lip service for young men who gave way too much for colonialism and the self-serving elite.

In Danny's mind he could also see his negative slugs who were hateful and greedy and driven by some insidious fear to resent his success. They were the slugs who were compelled to get appointments just so they could hold onto one of the best part-time jobs around. They had it all wrong. He could spot his negative slugs right away. Almost as if on cue, he overheard one of his slugs commenting to another slug about the awful school massacre in New England that happened on Friday the 14th.

The comment brought to Danny's recollection the conversation he had with Gray the night before. Gray told him that redneck guys often brought their guns to school to show them to other guys who thought guns were cool.

Danny clapped his hands together to release the energy he was feeling as he walked fast toward the front entrance of his building and out the front door into the cold December air without his coat. Faster and faster he walked, wanting to take Gray out of school right then and there—away from those idiots who bring guns to school. *This has to be done,* he reasoned to himself as he walked the six blocks to his car parked in the garage next to his apartment building.

During his drive to the school, he knew he was using the insane violence in New England to do this, and that his motive for driving to Gray's school was shaded by selfish material reasons that were partly related to running an independent business in America.

He stopped his route by turning around and heading back to Telemaster.

What Can I Do?

FOR THE THIRD day in a row, news about the New England school shooting flooded the television airwaves.

"Dad, why don't you run for president?"

"Oh, really! Because I have a business that works, I should run for the most stressful and important job on the planet? Why does every American ego think he has the brains or balls to be the president?" Danny asked with more than a trace of sardonic irony.

"Dad, you have ten thousand slugs who are subscribers to your *Peaceful Trails* newsletter. You know from your website and newsletter that over ninety percent of all slugs don't bother to vote because they're independents who don't like the choices that the system and the media validate."

"Well, what can I do?" Danny asked from his recliner above the news about New England on the television.

"RUN!" Gray yelled, which made his dad mute the TV with his remote.

Then Gray smiled at his dad and said, "Remember … when a slug's trailing, he's on the move.

Danny smiled and watched his son pace back and forth in front of the muted TV screen that showed policemen and government officials being interviewed about the tragedy.

Gray pointed at the muted screen that was showing the governor and president giving their condolences to the families of the tragedy. "Lip service, Dad! Sound familiar? You watch … I'll betcha all that really gets done will be a bunch of flags flying at half-staff! And then when the funerals are over, it'll be forgotten until the next idiot kills somebody. Lip service! NO ACTION!"

"What could the president do about this, Gray?" Danny was ready to debate his bright son.

"Well … for starters, Dad, he could get Congress to come back from vacation early to pass a bill to amend the Second Amendment. At least the country would know that something's being done. Martin Luther King, Jr. did it. Do you think those cronies would've done anything about Civil Rights without his action?"

"Good point, Gray. But again … what can I do?"

"Well, Dad, you've got ten thousand slugs who would listen to you. Get a hundred thousand. Organize them. Get them to show up at the White House for two days for a peaceful demonstration."

"Who at the White House cares about a bunch of

slugs?"

"Dad, you said many times that if slugs were organized and stopped working for any cause, the whole country would shut down."

"Then what's the cause?" his father pressed.

"Most people who don't carry a gun believe that our government is supposed to protect all of us from mentally ill people getting guns."

His father was ready to debate and asked, "What about alcohol and guns? How is the government going to stop anybody from drinking and getting their hands on a gun? Or wait! Forget about guns," Danny got out of his recliner. "What about drinking and driving? You can't stop that."

They stood in their living room looking at each other until Danny gestured for time out with his hands making a T as in a football game. "Okay … this is a country of laws," he said. "A big percentage of our politicians are lawyers entrenched in their party …"

"Oh, I get that, Dad," Gray interrupted. "We had a political science debate with a group of lawyers who work with state legislators in Lincoln. They agreed that the two political parties are locked into their own agendas, so nothing gets done. And they agreed that an independent presidential candidate has a better chance at getting elected than independents do at the state level. AND they all agreed that IF an independent was elected president, an army of voters three times the size of both parties would elect independents running for the Senate and Congress A-S-A-P."

"You're talking about amending the Second Amendment?"

"Yes," Gray nodded, adding, "Partisan politics does not work for three hundred million people with addictions and mental illnesses with a percentage of those having access to firearms and can kill children in grade schools. Come on, Dad … Even if you don't run, you can at least use your slugs to help support an independent who will."

"You're kidding me, right?" he asked his son, believing he was only practicing his debate skills.

Gray shook his head slowly from side to side. Then he said something that really intrigued his dad. He challenged Danny to let his slugs vote on it in his next *Peaceful Trails* monthly newsletter on the internet.

Danny sat down and leaned all the way back in his comfortable brown leather recliner with his hands locked behind his head. To Gray it looked like his dad was pondering his idea. The King of Slugs knew he didn't know anybody stupid enough to try such a thing. But the proposed rally of slugs in Washington had Danny's mind busy with all the angles, and he appeared to look right through his son when he said, "Yesterday I bought a new list of slugs along with their email addresses."

"How many slugs?" Gray asked with a thrilling intensity that he always got when his dad had a project for him.

"Fifty thousand."

Gray sat down at the desk in the living room in front of his dad's home computer and began typing on the keyboard until he pulled up on his screen the new file of the fifty thousand slugs. He swiveled around to his dad who was staring at the muted TV and absently going over a hundred details in his head about this proposed rally.

"Dad, you're the King of Slugs. You can get this done. Washington needs ... no, SLUGS NEED some kind of mass demonstration that the media has to cover. The president even said, 'We have to change.'" Gray watched his dad considering the thoughts in his mind, then he added, "I can get the word out so that every slug in America hears about our rally."

"Wait a minute. Just hold it there, buster," his dad was smiling with his palms extended out to Gray like a traffic cop.

"Dad, you're the one who said we'd do something 'crazy together' someday," Gray reminded him.

Danny looked long and lovingly at his son and chose his words carefully. "The rally really is a great idea now. The time is right to do something about gun control. But running for president, Gray ... come on! Do you think I'm that stupid?"

"No, I don't think you're stupid. I've seen how you run Telemaster. You get things done. That's why I know you'd make a great president."

"Running Telemaster is a far cry from running a country. That's too serious. I mean ... Commander-in-Chief ... come on! That's not me."

"That's just it, Dad. We need a president who runs the country like you run Telemaster. We need a president who keeps us out of wars."

"Lawyers in Congress run this country ..."

"An independent president can get things done because the same old cronies in Congress will be voted out, one right after the other, when the top man's an independent."

"Who says so?" he asked his son.

"Nobody has to SAY it, Dad. Somebody has to DO it. Then see what happens."

They stared at each other for a few moments until Gray said, "Why not at least organize a rally that wants the president to push to get amended gun laws passed … fast?"

"You realize what kind of logistics a rally like that would involve?"

"You could have the rally on some holiday that …"

"I don't know. Something big like that would have a bigger impact if it was on a workday … when people leave their work to make a statement."

"After Congress comes back from vacation," Gray surmised.

"Maybe." Danny's eyes revealed he was thinking, then he said, "Most slugs can't afford to miss work and go to Washington for two days, let alone pay for the transportation to and from there."

"What about buses? Everyone could chip in for gas and expenses. A thousand buses means about fifty-five thousand slugs. What would a thousand buses cost for such a rally?"

"Oh, Gray … there's so much more to putting together this kind of thing. I mean, the logistics of getting thousands of people together … They all need to eat and sleep … The bathroom logistics alone would be a nightmare!"

Father and son went back and forth discussing a thousand details that would need to be addressed in order to pull off something nearly impossible to fathom, let alone actually do.

Danny Mack, the King of Slugs, went to his bedroom just after midnight with the lambent, restless idea working ever so gently yet constantly on his busy mind. For a daunting hour during that winter-lonely time of night when sleep doesn't come easy and time moves faster than ever, he liked the whole idea of it—and the notion of finally making good on his promise to Gray to do something "crazy together."

Before sleep came for Danny, he could remember the very same words he'd asked God so many years ago when he first left his only child in California: *What can I do?* There was never an answer as far as he could tell. Not then, anyway. Yet the spirit of intent behind the question was for God to keep his boy safe from harm while he was so far away in Omaha.

Now, lying in the middle of his king-sized bed with his arms and legs spread out as far as possible, Danny was grateful that God had indeed kept his son safe and delivered him to Omaha. Danny remembered the pain of enduring many years of being only a summer dad who had managed to communicate with his son nearly every day of their lives after he left that madhouse he called California.

Every father has at least one memory of his child that can make him either laugh or cry. For Danny it was the day he left San Diego. He promised Gray, "I'll be there for you every day."

That's when little Gray asked, "Forever?"

"Yes … forever," he promised.

Now it was time to pay God back for Gray's safety for all those years. The answer to *What can I do?* was there on

Gray's face tonight when he reminded his dad he was the King of Slugs.

But what can I do about random violence by sick people? Those acts of violent madness that cause more and more families to die early, yet remain in a world haunted by what happened to their loved one? The senseless killings by guns ... by some crazy person ... by all of us, Danny mumbled to his tired mind.

Sleep finally came right after he vowed to a Higher Universal Power he called God, *I'm not waiting to be victimized by a lunatic before I do something about these mass killings with guns in my country.*

America is Fear

O N THEIR DRIVE to school the next morning, Gray and his dad saw three American flags at half-staff for the victims in New England. They saw a fourth flag flying at half-staff when Danny parked in front of Midtown High.

Gray started to open the passenger door after grabbing his backpack off the floor.

"Wait," Danny said.

Gray sat with his hand on the door handle and his face turned toward his dad.

"I know you're eighteen and I can't make you do this. I want you to clean out your locker and bring all your books to the principal's office. I need your help full time if we're going to Washington."

Gray's face lit up like Christmas morning. "You mean it?" he asked with an excited grin.

"You bet I do. Kids aren't safe in schools today. I'd rather see you homeschooled until you get your diploma. How's that sound to you?" Danny extended his fisted right hand and they knuckle-bumped before Gray got out of the car with his backpack.

The principal wasn't in, so Danny saw the vice principal and informed her, "I'm removing my son from school in order to keep him safe from harm in our violent society. American schools have been proven repeatedly to be places where kids can be trapped like animals and slaughtered."

The vice principal was very surprised by Danny's words and even more surprised to see a parent taking action. "Mr. Gray," she responded, obviously taken aback, "I can assure you we do everything allowable by law to ensure the safety of our students. You have no need to worry about your son's safety here at Midtown."

"Look, ma'am ... are you aware kids are bringing guns to school in their cars and showing them off to each other before and after school? Do you know which kids they are? Do you know if any of those kids are suffering from any mental illnesses ... diagnosed or undiagnosed?"

The vice principal just stood staring at Danny Mack with her mouth agape.

"I guess that answers my question. My son is not as safe as you seem to think he is."

Gray left all his text books on the front office counter after Danny had the vice principal give him a signed receipt that all the books assigned to him had been returned.

On their drive to Telemaster, Gray talked about how afraid many of the students and teachers were of the boys with reputations for being violent or skipping school often.

"America is fear," Danny declared. "It's the mentally unstable cowards with access to guns who fester with their own fears until they snap. The bullies and loudmouths have an outlet. At least you know where they're coming from. It's those quiet cowards who are ill who have to be monitored."

"Yeah … makes sense," Gray nodded, visualizing kids like that at school.

Danny continued, "I get tired of hearing from other students and relatives and neighbors of these cowards who say, 'He was so quiet and minded his own business,' or 'He was the last person I'd suspect.' Blah, blah, blah! I'm tired of the whole scene."

They drove a few miles in silence, then Danny changed the subject and said, "Okay, you're working for me now. I'll pay you three hundred a week to keep the phones and computers running, update the website and newsletter, and you handle all the tech support for the rally project that *may* happen on Martin Luther King Jr., Day."

"That's so cool, Dad!"

"When we get to Slug Central, I want you to get on your computer and find out all you can about homeschooling … getting your diploma. And you're paying for it out of your salary! That's your first priority, and I want a meeting with you this afternoon on your findings. Okay?"

"Okay," Gray smiled, excited to be working for his dad on a dream job he was starting without any notice.

"Oh," Danny added with an afterthought, "that one violent video game that you have?"

"I don't play it. It was a gift from my friend Carter when I left San Diego."

"Get rid of it. I don't want it in our home."

"Okay, Dad."

Inside busy Slug Central amidst the countless translucent partitioned cubicles, so many slugs waved and smiled at them. It amazed Gray to see the obvious love and respect his father received from his slugs. They really did appreciate Danny Mack. The father and son made their way to the center of their calling maze where Danny's office was located.

Most every day at work Danny could be seen pacing his office while on the phone with his headset wrapped over the top of his curly head. He liked to use the same phone and headset his slugs used. He took breaks with them and had lunch with them in the coffeehouse and café. Gray discovered early on that what really endeared this loyal army of part-time slugs was that his dad fought for and got an affordable healthcare plan for his non-smoking slugs. Over sixty percent of his long-term slugs smoked when they first started working for Telemaster. That number had dropped to eighteen percent because of the healthcare plan Danny managed to get for them when they stopped smoking.

Shelly greeted her boss and the new slug. "Hey, Gray! You skipping school today?"

Danny told Shelly, "Have Mary in Personnel bring all the forms for Gray to fill out. He's working for us now."

"Really? Welcome aboard!" she smiled at Gray's happy face.

Once inside Danny's office, Gray got right on the computer and started researching homeschooling. Danny sorted through his email on his laptop while sitting at the desk Gray had picked out for him two summers ago. He hated computers or anything more technical than a cell phone. He refused to ever send a text message. One time from their apartment window, Danny saw Gray texting while driving his car into the parking lot below, and he took his smart phone away from him for two weeks. It seemed harsh at the time; however, Danny had warned his son previously that there would be a penalty if he ever texted while driving.

Gray was a genius when it came to computers: programming, troubleshooting and repairing, building websites and designing software. Anything technical, whether a tool or a toy, Gray Mack would master it. Fast. He once tried to explain his uncanny abilities to his dad. "I don't really know how I do it. I just think about what I want to do and it comes to me … like in a dream."

Earlier in the fall when one of Gray's teachers was having trouble with salacious material being sent to him by hackers, Gray offered his help. In no time at all he found the hacker online and sent him a message that stopped the intrusions: "We know who you are. America is fear. You are one of its cowards."

Danny remembered Gray telling him about the hacker, and he told his son to start a list of slogans for the rally—slogans that could be carried and displayed on protest signs by demonstrators in Washington. Two slogans that Danny wanted were "America is Fear" and "Guns and Cowards Don't Mix."

The boss called out to his new slug, who was on the keyboard and squinting at the screen because he needed glasses and was resisting getting them, "You could have a graphic of an assault weapon and the word 'COWARD' in big bold yellow letters inside a red circle with a red slash through it … indicating guns and cowards not permitted."

"Yeah, that would be good," Gray thought as he typed away.

Before Danny could fully imagine what he'd just told Gray, already on the screen was the protest sign he had just described.

"Good! Looks good," his dad was amazed.

Danny checked his desk calendar and saw that the Martin Luther King, Jr. holiday was on the 21st of January.

"Gray?"

"Yeah," Gray answered, squinting at another slogan he was working on.

"Make a note. Send a Slug Alert to every workstation polling all employees, both shifts. 'Respond if interested in attending gun-control rally in D.C. Leaving Omaha the morning of Saturday the 19th of January, returning to work Wednesday the 23rd. Telemaster closed Monday because of the holiday. No pay for Tuesday. Telemaster pays all travel, food and lodging expenses. Feedback requested. Meeting today at end of each shift. All slugs on deck.' And put those protest signs around the text and give it to Shelly to edit. And Gray?"

"Yeah."

"Get your eyes checked."

By the time Shelly had the Slug Alert ready and sent, Burt was gathering information from charter bus companies after meeting with Danny about the proposed rally. "You do know it's January?" Burt asked cynically, knowing he'd be going along to the rally.

Within minutes every slug at every workstation read the Slug Alert regarding the rally. Paid expenses but no wages for one day. Danny was unsure about how his slugs would vote on the unique proposal posted on the alert. That's why the King of Slugs had Gray post that there would be an "all slugs on deck" meeting ten minutes before the end of each shift.

Prior to the first meeting, Burt was in Danny's office going over the figures his boss had requested. Gray and Shelly were sitting in on the meeting with Burt's wife taking copious notes.

"Twenty-four hundred dollars per bus roundtrip," Burt announced.

"Catered and travel food for four days?" Danny asked his accountant.

"About five grand per bus," Burt read from his notes.

"How about lodging?"

"About six grand per bus," Burt replied.

"So we're around twelve or thirteen grand per busload?" Danny asked.

"Right. And wages lost per busload is about three grand. Gross income lost if they all go to the rally is about three hundred grand."

Danny took a deep breath and looked at Gray as if to

say this was getting to be expensive. "Shelly, what did you find out about where we can stage the rally with or without a permit?"

"Lafayette Park is across the street from the White House. Permits are required in order to ensure toilet facilities are in the park. Metro Police will be there to ensure that sidewalks and streets are not obstructed … and that things don't 'get out of hand,'" she said using finger quotes.

Burt asked, "Why not hold the rally at the Capitol Building to send Congress a message? They're the ones who have to pass bills that create new laws. The president can't get anything done if an anti-gun-control Congress won't act on this."

"That's right," Shelly agreed.

That's when Danny had an idea and shared it with them by logically walking them through it. "You're right, it's going to be cold. *If* all three thousand slugs go, that's still not a big enough gathering … as far as the media's concerned, right?"

"Maybe," Burt said skeptically.

Then Gray said, "But what if each slug was on a cell phone or smart phone calling and texting the anti-gun-control politicians and letting them know something has to be done about these mentally unstable people who can murder kids in a school?"

"Assault weapons with high magazine counts have to be banned," Burt said.

"And mandatory background checks for everyone," Shelly asserted.

"Every time some mass shooting happens, the media's

all over it and the public start buying guns like crazy," Burt declared.

"America is fear," Danny smiled at his son.

"Cowards and guns don't mix," Gray smiled back at his dad.

Then Danny went on to proclaim, "It's not so much gun control that we need, we need conscious people control. Mentally ill people like that kid in New England shouldn't be able to get their hands on any gun … especially an assault weapon, for God's sake."

Shelly agreed with her boss, but then she said, "I read that two-thirds of Americans don't have any guns of any kind. Why can't that majority get organized and legislate some sanity into this issue?" Upon looking around the table for an answer from one of the three men she reasserted, "I'd really like to know."

Her boss answered, "I'll tell you why. The majority of Americans are not victims of a coward or sick person with a gun. Most people work too hard to pay their bills. They don't have time to organize, protest, or break away from their routines to get anything changed in this country. Fear is big money for millions of people who work for companies that sell fear to all of us to keep it all going. Insurance companies, lawyers, gun lobbyists, security systems, the police and court system, the MEDIA … We're the most heavily armed and drugged society on earth. Even our government *by far* is the world's biggest arms dealer. Our military takes way too much money to sustain itself. And things like poverty, education, and gun-control get lip service."

Gray pressed his dad and asked him what he would do

if he was the president.

"There's only one thing I would do. Instead of spending half my time campaigning and trying to work with those pinheads in Congress and getting nowhere, I'd get unregistered independent men and women to register and push for laws to make it easier to register to vote. Until this country kicks out the status quo … the same cronies who claim to represent us but only represent their own interests … we won't change or get anything done. The whole antiquated system is set up to resist change." Danny waved off his diatribe. "Back to the rally. Okay, if we do this rally, *what if* every slug had a cell phone or smart phone and was calling and texting every congressperson and every senator while in that park across the street from the White House? And *what if* on the way to this rally we called and texted every major media organization in this country? *What if* we did something like that?"

Danny looked around his office at his accountant, his secretary, and then his son. He could see on their faces that they were delighted to know he had a plan of action. And that he was willing to put his money on the line.

"I'm in, Dad."

Then cautious Burt said, "The question is will three thousand people give up sixty bucks to do this?"

Flags and Meetings

B Y 12:50 THAT same day, all 1,500 slugs from the 9:00 a.m. to 1:00 p.m. shift stood in one massive circle, surrounding their boss near the middle of Slug Central. The music playing above them was silenced by Gray. Danny turned 360 degrees as he spoke to his slugs circled all around him.

"As you saw on the Slug Alert, I want you to go home tonight and sleep on this rally idea, and then vote on it by the end of your shift tomorrow. If a majority of you vote yes, we go to Washington … those of you that want to go … and we make our voices heard on this gun-control issue. We're not talking about taking your guns away! We're talking about banning all assault weapons and keeping guns out of the hands of people who have no business getting access to any firearm. Loopholes at gun shows should be closed! Any of you who vote no on the rally and do not want stiffer gun control laws won't be forced to go on this journey … and you will be able to work your regular shift."

"What are you giving up?" an anonymous slug asked the boss.

"More than you," Danny fired back. "I know my losses are relative to yours since many of you live check to check and the loss of a day's pay really hurts. But I believe we should do something like this … and we'll always need money."

Another slug called out, "Why can't we call those people from here? Call a little bit every day … every shift? Why go all the way out there? It's January, Danny!"

"I've thought about that. We might call from here if we don't go. I thought we'd make a bigger impact by going there, in case they ignored our phone calls."

Another slug wanted to know who they'd be calling on a weekend and holiday.

"Switchboards … answering machines … media contact numbers. We'll pound 'em! Twenty-four hours of slugs pounding the phones of every politician in the country will get their attention. We've got to get something changed about our violent society. If we can help prevent even one of these massacres from happening, isn't it worth it?"

He looked at all his slugs and told them to vote tomorrow and to submit any slogan suggestions they might have to Shelly.

The same meeting with the afternoon shift took place at

4:50. Shelly, who was in charge of getting calling lists for clients, had to come up with a political calling list of every elected official in the country for slugs to call on the way to and while attending the rally.

Just an hour before the second meeting, Gray told his father how this could be the catalyst that would propel his father into the political spotlight for a future presidential bid.

"You may be right," Danny said, adding, "but it's way too early to think about that … don't you think?"

"Not really," Gray was serious as if he were anticipating his father's response and continued, "It's more late than early if you ask me. Democrats and Republicans need some real competition or they just grow bigger government … bigger corporations. Then it's the small businesses that are left to complain about the same broken system."

"How do you know all these things?" Danny asked his son.

"I know that any rally is just more lip service if some kind of political action doesn't come from it."

"Do you have any idea how much it would take to do such a thing?"

"A lot less than the others spend. And that's what slugs really want to see … a party that can be put together without spending much. No TV ads. That's what slugs will vote for."

"You have no idea what that could cost," Danny fired back at his naïve new employee.

"Yeah, but what's the cost if we don't try?" Gray shot back in all seriousness.

Danny began pacing around his office, now and then looking through the mint-green glass of his walls to his slugs calling prospects from their clear cubes.

"What's wrong, Dad?"

"They won't go for it," Danny said while shaking his head from side to side.

"What do you mean?"

"They won't vote for it. Sixty bucks is more important to them."

"How do you know?" Gray was curious.

"I saw it on their faces. Less than half of them were on board with it."

"Maybe there's something more you can say to the second shift that motivates them to want to go. And if it helps … I can put it on the website for the first shift to see.

By the time the second meeting was over, again Danny saw that his slugs just weren't on board with it—that their lost wages was too much to give up. And Gray saw it too.

On their short drive home Gray summed up the second meeting. "You were more passionate. I mean, when you said, 'I can't do this without you,' really, Dad, I felt your passion … and so did they."

"And then what did you see?' Danny asked his bright son.

"I saw what you saw after the first meeting. The money."

"Yeah, and then at the end I even said, 'Everyone here *has* to give up something to help a greater cause if you want change to happen."

"Yeah, that was good. But like you said … it's about

the money."

"Right," Danny banged the palm of his hand on his steering wheel to show his frustration as they cruised down Tenth Street toward home.

The dark streets of winter in downtown Omaha were blue-black, dirty and slushy in the aftermath of the two inches of snow two days earlier. They pulled into their parking lot and entered their covered garage parking stall, a winter sanctuary connected to their building. When his dad turned off his engine Gray said, "I'm certain you can still make an impact on gun control without leaving Omaha."

"How's that?"

"One of your slugs hit on it at the first shift meeting. You could have every slug who supports the issue make a few calls from Telemaster every day to congressional members and senators. That way they wouldn't lose pay, and you would save the freakin' expensive long trip to D.C. I really think it can be a more cost-effective way to make a difference." Gray watched in silence as his dad took in the idea.

Soon Danny admitted, "That's not a bad idea."

"And you would still be at least trying to do something about it."

Danny was thinking out loud when he said, "Our calls could make a difference."

"It's a lot easier, Dad … and it would save a fortune. Even the slugs who vote against going to the rally might still make calls from here 'cause they won't lose any wages."

"We'll still have to vote on it," Danny said.

"I could put out a Slug Alert and add an amendment to the vote. Like option two is calling from Telemaster ..."

"No, I still want to see how the voting goes without an alternative plan. It'll tell us a lot."

"Yeah, I see your point" Gray agreed.

Gray and Danny had one continuous meeting from the time they sat down to eat dinner until bedtime when the outside temperature dipped below zero for the first time that winter in Omaha. Lying wide awake in their rooms, both father and son were excited about their "Plan Be," as Gray called it, where each slug would make no more than ten quick calls to politicians every shift.

While Danny kept going over the numbers in his head, Gray was excited to be working with his dad. He was thrilled to be out of school and doing something "real" with his life. He had told his dad earlier in the evening that he could get his high school diploma by taking a GED exam.

"Then do it ... soon," his father implored. "That way we don't have to deal with your mother when she finds out I took you out of school."

Around 11:30 as winter winds blew howling whistles through the cracks around Gray's bedroom window, he could stand it no longer. He went to his computer to read any email responses from his dad's newsletter or responses from slugs at work—any feedback about the issue of gun control.

Meanwhile, Danny had opened his bedroom window to breathe a blast of cold December air to clear his busy mind. That's when he heard the two dozen or so ConAgra

American flags flapping in the wind at half-staff, an ominous reminder that showed the country's respect for the kids and teachers killed and injured in New England. *Flags and meetings ... Is that all we'll get?* he wondered with a cynical snort of contempt for the unwillingness of the country's leadership to even give the appearance that something would be done to diminish the chances of these kinds of massacres from happening again.

Danny continued listening to the massive flags. Their combined red, white and blue fabric snapped and flapped, and their wind-made noise was louder than he'd ever heard before. It was a cacophony of noise that only flags can make. *Then why not make our noise as a nation?* he continued with his thoughts. *If another country or terrorists had done this to our schoolchildren, we'd declare war and make them pay a thousand times over with our blood and treasure. But this ... from within ... one murderous act ... and over ten thousand more murders a year one at a time ... in a country where it's possible for mentally ill people to kill. And all the angry and stupid gangs and boyfriends and repeat criminals with records of violence ... they're all inch-brow cowards who have to be stopped. Let 'em use knives and clubs and beat their angry fists on flesh and give us a fighting chance against their pain and anger.*

He stopped his inward diatribe and appeased his mind knowing that in his little world of Gray and himself, at least he'd made a move and took action by removing Gray from harm's way in a school where every year a few guns are brought to school by idiots and shown to their friends to impress them. Gray said they would be locked in their cars. Not for protection. Not for anything more than a fearful mind that requires a gun to feel more safe.

Danny and his angry mind moved to another negative thought. *Tomorrow the voting will be in by the end of the second shift. They won't approve it, I know.*

He closed his bedroom window, hopeful that sleep would come fast now that the metallic sound of the flags was no longer audible.

Gray was still wide awake in front of his monitor reading emails concerning the upcoming vote. They were mostly comments directed to his father and other slugs about to vote on the rally.

"Hey, King of Slugs! It's FR-FR-FReezing C-Cold out there!"

"Slug Alert! Vote NO!"

"Slugs can't move at all when it's that cold!"

"SLUGS HAVE THE RIGHT TO PROTECT THEIR LOVED ONES! Vote NO!"

"YES! VOTE YES TOMORROW! LET'S ALL DO SOMETHING FOR ALL OUR KIDS IN SCHOOL!"

"At least we can do this for our violent society that I know we are all responsible for, since our politicians reflect our collective insanity."

"Yay! Let's roll with our king to D.C. and show 'em all what slugs can do."

"If we start taking guns away from people, we'll be at the mercy of criminals who obtain guns illegally."

"There needs to be more of a background check that protects our children."

"WE'LL FREEZE OUR FRIGGIN' ASSES OFF!"

"It's too much $ to spend for buses when we can call

those deadbeats from here."

Gray agreed with the last email. He put his computer to sleep before getting into bed. He lay there in the soundless night thinking how lucky he was to be in Omaha with his father, and how he planned to take his GED test so that he could devote his energy to Telemaster and the rally—or whatever his boss wanted. He rubbed his tired eyes and reminded himself he had to get glasses with his first paycheck because his vision was affecting his ability to work on the computer.

The poster his dad had bought for him when he was ten was framed and hung above his headboard. He couldn't see Albert Einstein's face in the darkness, but knew that his quote on the poster applied more than ever to his father's work today: "Great spirits have always encountered violent opposition from mediocre minds."

Plan Be

B Y THE END of the second shift on "Slug Wednesday" the voting was all in. Shelly came into Danny's office with the voting results that she and Burt had verified. Gray looked up from his computer screen and the boss dropped what he was doing at his desk. Danny's secretary and accountant sat down across from him to give him the results.

Danny was jaded. "Don't tell me," he said. "Let me guess. About three-to-one against."

Shelly and Burt looked at each other, amazed at how close Danny's guess was to the results: Twenty-four percent had voted yes, seventy-six percent were against.

Then Danny asked what he wanted to know from notes he'd made. "How many voted?"

"Ninety-eight percent ... just over twenty-nine

hundred votes," Burt read from his notes.

"Any noticeable disparity in the shifts?"

"No," Burt shook his head.

That told Danny's analytical mind that his pitch to the first shift wasn't any better or worse compared to the second shift. That was all the accountant could tell his boss since the individual voting was one hundred percent confidential. Danny introduced to his staff "Plan Be," which would be put in the newsletter and on the website letting all employees and 10,621 subscribers know that Telemaster slugs who wanted to call politicians in Washington could make no more than ten calls per shift—anonymously, of course—demanding that something be done about assault weapons and pushing for the implementation of thorough background checks for all legal purchases of firearms, including all private transactions. Burt was told to post the voting result numbers on the website.

Gray was glad that slugs who wanted to could call elected officials to compel them to do something about making our country less violent. He was elated to be away from those boring classrooms of rote learning. He knew that his dad would make a good president because of his ability to bring people together and work out their differences. And he was excited about his new role at Telemaster. *Could an independent man like my dad win the highest office in 2016?* he wondered. *I could put his name and face all over the internet without spending much money.*

Danny Mack had no real desire to run for president. He

was aware that registered independent voters and apathetic unregistered slugs were too hard to capture—unless they could phone in their vote, and that would never happen.

He began drafting an article for the upcoming *Peaceful Trails*.

> *As we stand on the threshold of 2013, America's pulse beats too fast for any conscious change to happen. We must slow down and work smarter on the real problems we have ignored generation after generation.*

Danny stopped writing on his tablet while reposed in his recliner. CNN was muted and Gray was in his room working on the next Slug Alert and the layout for the next *Peaceful Trails*. After voting on Plan Be tomorrow, Danny was confident that at least seven hundred slugs would make calls every day on behalf of gun control.

Danny thought back to the Virginia Tech Massacre in 2007 and how Gray had told him that at his middle school in San Diego he started a slogan, "Cowards with Guns Kill." Gray also told his dad how his peers in school who were known to be violent resented and resisted his slogan to the point that he had to avoid several fights with these boys. They were aggressive and inclined to be pro-military.

Now that Danny had options, he was not going to let his only child be exposed to the unconscious ignorance of parents who allowed their kids to take a weapon to school.

At the next meeting near the end of the first shift, the King of Slugs could almost see every slug who had voted against the rally. His words surprised them.

"You were right. The rally wasn't a good idea. But the cause is! Now, for Plan Be ... as in 'Be Interested!' Plan Be is making a maximum of ten calls per shift, a quick call to elected men and women, both at their offices in Washington D.C. and at offices in their home states, telling them we want something done about these massacres by angry, violent, and sick people among us. We don't need to mention guns, the NRA, or amending the Second Amendment. We want them to make and pass laws that protect all of us. We want the violence to diminish! Whoever doesn't want to make these calls does NOT have to. I won't hold it against any slug who doesn't want to call. And those who do call don't have to make ten calls. Ten is the maximum number of calls you can make without hurting our clients' calling time. A call or two is also fine. Because the legislature is in recess for the Christmas break right now, we'll start making calls on Monday, January 7. I know that timing is everything ... and this is the right time to make a difference! So think about it and we'll vote on it on tomorrow."

From the crowd one slug asked, "Why do we have to vote on this? If we want to, we make some calls. If not, we don't!"

"I suppose we don't have to vote," Danny responded. "I was just trying to get a fix on how many would call. We don't have to vote. We could track the calls anyway and have the numbers to call on your screen at your station. Those who want to call, call!"

By the end of the second shift's meeting, all of the company's slugs knew that they could start calling politicians in early January if they wanted to. Gray was able to make sure on their phone system that no more than ten calls per shift were made. Gray was able to monitor individual slugs calling from their workstations, and every slug was aware of that.

Plan Be was set to begin right away on Monday, January 7, and the Macks were looking forward to playing a role in their country's gun-control movement.

*   *   *

January 7, 2013, dawned cold, but Danny was excited that the long-awaited day had arrived. Telemaster slugs were able to make ten calls to any of the D.C. and home state phone numbers listed on their computer's screen. Gray was able to see how many slugs were calling the offices of elected officials and even monitor the recorded calls that were made. Danny didn't want to know exactly who was calling; he was satisfied that he was part of something being done to protect all American citizens from criminals and/or the mentally ill who were contributing to making America the most violent country on earth.

After the first shift Gray informed his boss that forty-two percent of his slugs had made an average of eight calls to politicians. Roughly five thousand total calls had been made. After the end of the second shift, the numbers were pretty much the same.

"So we made about ten thousand calls today?" Danny

asked and received his son's nodding agreement. "Find out if we've maintained our level of appointments for our clients today."

Danny was surprised that his comptroller had an answer in fifteen seconds: "Two percent fewer appointments were set today."

"For both shifts?"

"Yes."

"I want those appointment figures every day by the end of the second shift."

"Okay."

Gray was well aware that his dad wanted to maintain the number of appointments set for each doctor during a billing period while the gun-control calls were made. Danny wasn't really worried if the numbers dropped a little bit, since most of his clients were happily forced to grow their practices in order to keep up with the consistent flow of new patients that Telemaster slugs generated.

Since each shift had floor managers who monitored and maintained the number of appointments set for their clients, these shift managers were trained to put one or two more slugs telemarketing for that particular client who had a lower-than-usual appointment ratio made for the calling period. Eventually more appointments would be set, and the client was happy.

Danny's slugs had so much experience telemarketing businesses for chiropractors that he knew exactly how many appointments should be set for the number of calling hours that the client prepaid. Telemaster continually rotated two hundred of its most experienced slugs—ten at a time—to find new clients. Their job was to keep all three-thousand-plus employees working at maximum capacity. And they did.

It took Telemaster ten of its twelve years in business before it was fully computerized with speed-dialing capabilities from a list viewed on a computer screen. "Quality appointments" was the company credo. If any slug set weak appointments consistently, that slug would be retrained and given another chance to set quality appointments. Usually that worked. If it didn't, it was "adios amigo." Danny Mack was aware that one bad slug would lose clients and have a deleterious effect on his service. There was no excuse for weak appointments. That didn't mean that the slug could be blamed for every appointment set that resulted in a no-show for the new-patient special. The same pros in the sales staff would verify every appointment made by every slug at Telemaster. These pros knew a bad slug upon verifying enough of their appointments, and one of those pros would be the one who retrained the weak slug because that particular pro would know exactly the kind of appointments the weak slug in question was setting. It was a beautiful quality control everyone respected and appreciated. Especially the clients.

*   *   *

Friday evening after the first week of "gun-control" calls to Washington, Gray was in his room listening to a batch of randomly recorded calls. The boss said it was one of his duties to monitor those calls, listening for any "problem slugs" who may be delivering a different message.

A typical call was short and sweet. The caller stated he or she wanting something done *now* about random violence with assault weapons and tougher background checks for the mentally ill.

Upon hearing several "normal" calls during a recorded batch from the first shift, one male slug's voice got his attention. "I'm in this boiler room in Omaha. Our boss is having a bunch of telemarketers call politicians and leave messages about gun control. Just thought you should know that these callers aren't in your voting district and we all don't feel that way. I wouldn't pay much attention to these calls. Just thought you should know."

That call was followed by another call made by the same anti-gun-control slug to another politician's office in Washington that was on the calling list.

Danny was meditating in the front room of their apartment to Northcore's song "Looking Glass" coming from cable's Soundscapes.

"Dad?" Gray interrupted him.

Danny opened his relaxed eyes.

"I think you should hear something … now."

Danny listened to all ten calls his anonymous slug made during his shift that were counter-productive to Danny's gun-control intention. Gray told him, "This slime ball made fifty calls the entire week to members of congress and senators." Danny knew the word would spread to all of the politicians on the list and nullify all the calls they'd made.

"You want to know who made the calls?" Gray asked his dad.

Slippery Trail

GRAY SPENT ALL weekend listening to over a thousand slugs who had made calls to Washington that first week. Of all the slugs, there was only one who delivered the wrong message—as far as Gray and his dad were concerned. Danny didn't recognize the voice of this particular "rat slug" who had been working at Telemaster for only two months. His name was Darin Bain. He was a thirty-nine-year-old slug from Bellevue, divorced with two young girls. Since all Telemaster prospective employees were given a mandatory drug test and criminal background check, Danny looked into Bain's personnel file and found out that he had been court-ordered in Nebraska to pay child support one month before starting at Telemaster. He could see also from the personnel records that no child support was being withheld from Bain's wages, so Danny couldn't tell for certain if his slug was supporting his kids out of his wages from Telemaster. The King of Slugs found himself torn between Bain's financial responsibility to his kids and his own desire to get rid of the rat who ruined their calling campaign for gun control, which now would have to be stopped on Monday because of Bain's selfish actions.

"One rotten apple ruined the whole project," Danny complained to his son.

"You going to fire him?" Gray asked his dad after he clicked out of Bain's personnel file on the computer screen.

"Not yet. I want you to track down his ex-wife so I can talk to her. I want to find out whether or not he's supporting his kids. If not, I'll garnish his wages and make sure he pays his child support. If he quits because I garnish his wages … good riddance. If not, at least I have the satisfaction of knowing his kids are being supported. But I can't fire him just because he's anti-gun-control."

"But why would you want a scumbag like that working for you?"

"I don't. But this is a country of laws."

"And no justice," Gray added.

Before the first shift started making calls on Monday morning, Gray had the gun-control calling list removed and posted a memo stating, "All calls to politicians have been suspended. Good job!"

Although Danny was disappointed to stop the calling

for gun control, he also had seen the appointment numbers for his clients drop three percent below the average by the end of the last week. He felt that his commitment to his clients was being compromised by taking thousands of calls away from them—even if it was for a good cause.

Now, as the boss walked around Slug Central, he purposely made his way over to Darin Bain's cube, wanting to see this "bad apple" he did not want working for him. Danny Mack was a pro at sizing up people, especially the self-serving, attitudinal, or underproductive slugs he'd worked with over the years. He was aware that slugs were not appreciated by most Americans; yet he more than anyone respected the good slugs who were bright and honest hard workers. These were men and women usually living a low-income lifestyle and often working two jobs to make ends meet.

He had his son check Bain's appointment ratio since working at Telemaster. It was good. A little above average, in fact. But still, for one of his slugs to make those snake-like calls to sell out his gun-control calls to the politicians was unconscionable. Yes, the King of Slugs was looking for one good reason to fire the snake in the grass who ruined the good work of so many.

Seated in his cube and talking into his headset was Darin Bain. Danny could see only Bain's back. His yellow-blonde hair was short and tapered. From Danny's vantage point he could see that Bain was maybe six feet tall and dressed casually in clean jeans and a shirt, which most of his slugs wore. The boss walked by Bain's cube and could see the profile of the slimy slug who ruined a small way of making a difference in this violent country where men like Bain preferred to be armed and ready if their government tried to take their guns away. Another quick look and then the boss was able to hear Bain during one of his calls. Danny was confused because the man appeared to be into his call, positive and animated, and even appeared to be a likeable looking and sounding young man. He left the area unseen by Bain, knowing that he only had one option left. He had to find out for certain if he was paying his child support at all.

Gray found out that Bain used his ex-wife as a reference, along with her work phone number. Danny called the number from his desk and was surprised that his ex-wife, Renee, worked at the Grand Avenue Café in Council Bluffs, a breakfast and lunch spot Danny used to frequent when he first moved to the area.

Danny put in a call to the café. When the hostess answered he asked, "Can you please tell me if Renee Bain works there?"

"Yeah, she does," the hostess answered. "Just a minute and I'll get her for you."

Without waiting for Renee to come onto the line, Danny hung up and went for his coat and wool cap hanging on the coatrack by his office door.

"Can I go along?" Gray asked.

"No. You get your GED handled."

Danny walked home, got his car and drove over to Council Bluffs—a familiar midsized Iowa city that always seemed to him to be a drab and dreary skirl of blown papers and stained streets seemingly peopled by hopeless survivors who'd just limped away from a bad accident.

Always when crossing into Council Bluffs, Danny thought of those exciting early days of Telemaster. This was the town where he began his climb—inching his way call by call out of a dark past in San Diego to Telemaster today. It was here in this place that he openly proclaimed his title as King of Slugs in order to be regaled as the best at one thing. Every man must believe he has some skill or talent or edge in order to get a foothold on the unstable, elusive ladder of opportunity that can lead him to success and prosperity in his line of work.

As he made his way along the familiar stretch of Broadway, the first month of 2013 was halfway gone. Already the media was turning its attention away from gun violence and focusing on inaugurations, debt ceilings, and unemployment figures. Moving along the bleak, frozen streets of this river city known for its railroad history, Danny marveled at Council Bluff's resignation to live in the shadow of Omaha. In its heyday Council Bluffs supplied all the materials that would build Omaha across the river into a city twelve times the size of Council Bluffs. Today Omaha stands as one of the financial behemoths of Middle America. Years ago someone in the Grand Avenue Café had joked to Danny that this working-class town was still Republican because the young politician Abe Lincoln had visited Council Bluffs railroad magnate Granville Dodge.

The Grand Avenue Café was located three blocks from the Dodge House, the very place where Honest Abe visited when he came to Council Bluffs to discuss the best location for a railroad distribution center. Danny could see the grand house as he pulled into the back parking lot of the café. Once he was out of the car, he turned toward the Loess Hills and again could see the historical landmark that overlooked the city. He recalled how he and Gray toured the house on one summer vacation.

Gray was on his mind now. For most of his son's life he'd been promising him that they'd spend more time together once he graduated from high school. "That's when we'll do something crazy together," Danny promised his son.

When he turned back and headed for the café's back entrance, his negative thoughts about Bain, the slug who had betrayed his confidence, were propelling his quick steps across the frozen snow-mashed pavement of the parking lot. He stomped the frangible chunks of snow from his shoes and entered the café door, just as he had done a hundred other times when he was a struggling slug here.

Once inside the brightly lit, clean café with its polished antique oak high-back booths, Danny realized he hadn't given a thought to what he would say to Bain's ex-wife. He couldn't be his extemporaneous self when he dialed a phone number; this was something else.

It came to him when he took his seat. He decided to play it straight and not use chicanery. His waitress was friendly and took his order for coffee and apple pie with vanilla ice cream. It was a treat he'd give himself every Friday at the end of his week before he moved his business to Omaha.

"You want me to warm up your pie a little?" she asked.

Danny nodded yes. As his waitress stepped away, he went over in his mind what he would say to Bain's ex-wife. He thought about lying and telling her he was from Social Services in order to get information, but Danny prided himself on being a man of honesty and integrity. When his order arrived, he simply asked if Renee was in.

"Yes, she's in the kitchen," the waitress replied.

"Any way I could speak with her for a few minutes? It's important."

The waitress smiled and walked back toward the kitchen area.

Danny spooned some ice cream into his coffee and stirred it a bit, swirling the black liquid to a butterscotch color—another thing he used to do here every Friday afternoon. He looked up and saw who must be Renee Bain exiting the kitchen and looking his way while walking toward his table. She appeared unsure of who this man was and what he wanted. Danny reached for his glasses that were stored in a case inside his coat pocket beside him; he wanted to see more clearly this woman in order to gauge and size-up everything he could about her. She was brunette and brow-beaten attractive, obviously a single mother struggling to support her kids. Her eyes were fearful at first until he extended his hand and in a relaxed tone of voice asked her to please sit down. "I'm Danny Mack. Your ex-husband, Darin, works for me at Telemaster in Omaha."

He saw fear and wariness in her eyes, as if fearing something Darin had done—or could yet do.

Danny continued, "Our personnel records show that Darin has a court order to pay you child support. Has he been paying you?"

Her eyes revealed fear, uncertain what to say to Darin's boss, a man she heard was a successful businessman. Then she told Danny the truth, that he had never paid any support.

"Uh-huh," Danny nodded and sipped off the remaining ice cream floating on top of his coffee. "How much did the court order Darin to pay you a month?"

"Two hundred and sixty dollars."

"For two kids, right?"

She nodded yes.

"Boy, that's not much. Did he say why he isn't paying you?"

"He won't ever pay me, Mr. Mack. Look ... he hates me and I hate him. He's not the kind of man to own up to his responsibilities."

"I see," Danny nodded while ladling more melted ice cream from his pie into his coffee. "I know that several of my slugs ... I mean employees ... have money garnished from their wages to pay their child support. I noticed that Darin is using four deductions on his W-4 form, claiming you and your kids. That means he's taking home more money every payday ... prob'ly around four hundred fifty every two weeks. Do you know if he has another job?"

"He works under the table doing handyman work. I think he works off his rent doin' maintenance for the apartment building he lives in."

Danny nodded while taking his first bite of his apple pie.

"May I call you Renee?"

She nodded yes.

"Renee, does Darin visit your kids?"

"Never. He says it's my fault he doesn't come and see the kids since I moved in with my mom. He hates her, too."

"I see. I can have his wages garnished right away … so you'll get at least one month of back support next Friday. I can make sure that happens, but I'm afraid he'll quit working at Telemaster when he finds out his child support has been taken out of his check."

She agreed with a nod and kept quiet until she had to tell this nice man who was trying to help her, "Mr. Mack … I appreciate it, but I don't want you to garnish Darin's check. He's a violent man and I don't want any trouble. Like you say, he'll just quit … but he'll think I made you garnish his wages. He could get real crazy drunk and cause me and my kids trouble."

"I see," Danny's eyes understood, and then he said just before taking another bite of pie, "This is a slippery trail 'cause I really want him to pay you child support. That's the only way I'll let him work for me. Otherwise, I'll fire him."

"All the court orders in the world won't make him pay me. He's too selfish. You should just fire him, then."

Danny leaned forward and said, "Renee, look … I'll take two hundred and sixty out of his check this Friday and write you a check now for two hundred and sixty. When he goes to our personnel office, I'll let Payroll know to tell him that Social Services notified us of the child support order, and we garnished his wages. He'll prob'ly quit right then … but at least you'll get a month's support from him. He'll never know I talked to you. I promise."

Renee sat looking into this man's gray eyes and said.

"He's gonna be real pissed. Money is a god to him. I think he's bipolar or somethin' because he gets crazy and weird and won't go to a doctor."

"It's your money. You can tell him you didn't even get a check yet from Social Services if he talks to you Friday. Play his game, Renee. Tell him, 'What check?' Right? If he doesn't quit, I'll have a hundred and thirty bucks taken out of his pay that he gets from me every two weeks. I won't stand for anyone workin' for me who doesn't help support his kids. You have two girls, right?"

"Uh-huh," she smiled.

"How old are they?"

"Seven and eleven."

"Seven, eleven … two lucky numbers, huh?" he smiled and leaned back after scooping another spoonful of melted ice cream into his coffee. "So … you prob'ly have to get back to work. Can I write you a check for two hundred sixty?"

"Sure … if you're sure he won't find out."

"I guarantee it." He got out his checkbook and wrote her a check.

Danny watched her walk back to the kitchen, telling himself, *Well, I helped her at least get one month of child support from that selfish bastard.* As he finished his dessert, he wondered if he should talk to Bain and let him know how bad it could be for his daughters and himself psychologically if he didn't pay his child support. Maybe he should advise his attitudinal employee that he should try to be a positive person for their sake. But then he could still see how scared Renee looked when she imagined her ex-husband's response to being forced to give her his precious money.

*　　*　　*

Arriving back at work, Danny parked in his reserved parking space near the main entrance to Telemaster. He felt better about helping Renee get some money. Now all he had to do was wait until Friday, and he felt certain Bain would quit. Yet the memory of Bain's voice calling the politicians and warning them about the calls from Telemaster was still a sore spot.

Purposely Danny took a different route to his office in order to see Bain at his workstation. He was making his calls and appeared to be happy that the calls to the politicians had stopped. Danny wanted to go into his cube, remove Bain's headset from his empty skull, and boot his ass out of his building. But he couldn't. *Too many lawyers and no justice,* he reminded himself.

Danny gazed up and smiled at the company mascot, the giant snail turning ever so slowly with the company motto, "Slow down … there's plenty of time." He reminded himself that legally he couldn't take money out of Bain's check for child support, but he didn't trust the system to handle it. *This is the right thing to do … and quick, like justice should be,* he told his mind.

Believing he had done a good deed for Renee and her kids—and gotten a little revenge for Bain's calls to Washington—Danny could now let it go because he had taken the action needed to set things right.

Payday

THE EARLY MID-JANUARY morning had warmed to forty degrees in the Omaha area. It was Friday, payday at Telemaster. This was the payday that Gray was to get his new glasses after getting his eyes examined the week previous. Thursday afternoon Gray had taken the first of his GED exams and passed, so he and his father were elated to have that behind them.

Thursday night Gray had created graphics on his computer for the upcoming *Peaceful Trails* newsletter. He talked to his dad about putting visual graphics that would encourage members to call their congressional representatives demanding action to decrease violence by firearms in our country. It was Gray's idea to list each state's senators and congressional representatives, along with their phone numbers in Washington, in order to make it easier for constituents to call.

For the last three nights, Danny had been organizing his ideas to post in the February newsletter. He composed a proposal that he thought would diminish the gun violence in America. It consisted of three distinct ideas that he wanted feedback on from members:

1. Extensive background checks by Homeland Security for anyone buying a firearm legally, including mandatory registering of any private sale or trading of firearms by individuals.

2. Make it a federal offense for anyone who commits a crime while using any kind of firearm, with mandatory jail time and longer sentences for the offenses.

3. Build a massive federal penitentiary in Alaska to incarcerate and rehabilitate felons who commit crimes with firearms. This punishment would be known as "one strike, you're in."

To elaborate on each of his ideas, he wrote in his newsletter:

> *To be carrying any firearm with bad intentions anywhere that unarmed people gather is cowardly and should be dealt with as severely as any terrorist act. All people have the right to be free from cowards with bad intentions.*
>
> *Cowards who commit crimes with firearms should fear the consequences and pay severely. These fear-driven cowards diminish our right to live well and in safety. Many of these cowards are the same repeat*

criminals who continue moving in and out of our broken court system where justice is not serving law-abiding citizens who are repeatedly victimized by these cowards.

Let them all know that "one strike, you're in" means they will be locked up in Alaska—far away from visitors and with no hope for an early release date because of state budgets and over-crowded conditions. This will leave states with more revenue to deal with other criminals and the mentally ill.

If these three ideas can be approved by a referendum of voting Americans in a democratic society, there will be a growing consciousness and shift toward peace, harmony, and justice for all. That's the kind of America I want to live in. There are too many addicts in America and too many sick people with no business getting access to a firearm.

America is the largest arms dealer on the planet, and our citizens are by far the most heavily armed. We must begin drawing lines and at least be conscious enough to know that some of us are dangerous to all of us. Our people have a civil right to be safe from an outdated Second Amendment. Today we have more men in prisons than what was the entire population of the country back when the Second Amendment was created. In a lousy prison system with a high rate of *recidivism, we must be willing to educate and train these people who were failed by an absence of good parenting.*

If just one mentally ill person, one angry person in a rage, or one repeat felon is stopped from killing or injuring one person in this country because of thorough background checks; or if one gun dealer or individual—legal or otherwise—thinks twice about selling a firearm because of stricter firearm registration laws and longer prison sentences; then at the very least it's worth it.

Because of one bad apple or slug, I am unable to have any willing employees campaign for gun-control laws. So I'm asking for your input without coopting or doing nothing because of one idiot who is part of the problem.

That was the rough draft Shelly would edit for the February *Peaceful Trails* that would be coming out in a few days. Meanwhile, Gray was finishing his work on the graphic design for the same newsletter. He wanted to show his work to his dad before they left for work, but they were sidetracked at breakfast when Gray's mother called from San Diego wanting to know how things were going for Gray in school. Gray wasn't good at lying so he told his mother, "I have taken and passed one of my GED tests and will take another one today. I'm working for Dad now instead of going to school."

That's when she asked to talk to Danny.

Gray went to his room not wanting to hear the conversation between his parents, but he could hear it anyway. He heard his dad explaining, "After the New England shooting last month, I didn't want Gray exposed to an unsafe situation. There are big problems with gang violence in Omaha. I'm not going to sit around and wait for something bad to happen, so I took him out of school."

Gray could tell his dad was listening to his mother's diatribe and was happy when he finally said to his mother, "Well, he took one of his tests and passed it, and he will be taking the second one this afternoon. Within a month he should have his diploma. He's working for me now … AND HE LOVES IT!"

After another long silence his dad continued, "Yes, that's right! As you know he's quite good with computers, and he's working full time. *If* he wants to go to college he can! … I know. … I know. I'll send you a copy of his diploma when he gets it. … Okay. … Bye."

Gray came out of his room dressed for work, expecting to hear negative feedback about his mother's call. All Danny said was that his mother wanted a copy of his diploma when he got it. Gray was aware that it was hard for his mother to give up the child support his dad didn't have to pay her now; however, he also knew he may have dropped out of school in San Diego because he was bored with school. He hated living with his mom and her new husband, and he wanted to live with his dad in Omaha.

They drove to work that morning because Gray was taking the second of his GED tests and picking up his new glasses later in the afternoon. Once inside Telemaster,

Danny veered off his usual route to his office and made his way to Bain's cube. The morning shift had already begun, and the slugs would have had their paycheck envelopes waiting for them on their desks when they arrived to work. Just as the boss figured, Bain's chair was empty. He stepped inside Bain's cube, and on Bain's desk he could see the opened and empty pay envelope. The top of his desk was barren except for an empty coffee mug. A smile came to Danny when he thought about how he'd gone into Payroll after his meeting with Renee and told Jerry, the payroll clerk, to take out $260.00 from Bain's pay, and that Bain would probably be coming in to find out why his check was short the $260.00.

"Tell him it's for back child support, and that every payday from now on $150.00 will be taken out until he is caught up," Danny advised "Once he's current, we'll take out $130.00 per check for the ongoing support."

"Can you do that?" Jerry asked his boss.

"No ... but let that worthless deadbeat sue me. I've made sure his ex-wife gets the money. Since the State of Nebraska hasn't bothered to find him here and hold him accountable ... I will."

Making his way along the maze of cubes across the massive main floor of Slug Central, Danny kept his eyes peeled for that snake who had ruined all those calls to the politicians. Bain could be in Jerry's Payroll office now, or maybe he'd just left. Peeking into the Payroll office, Danny could see that Jerry was alone and on his phone in his office. The boss sat down across from Jerry's desk. Jerry got off his call fast.

"Bain?" Danny said.

"He was here … and quite upset," Jerry complained with more than a trace of cynical irritation."

"Did he quit?"

"I would say so. You know, if he goes to the State's Attorney with this, we can be fined."

"He won't go to the State's Attorney. That's the last place that scumbag would go. And if he does … I'll handle it."

When Danny stood up he asked Jerry what Bain said to him.

"He asked me why his check was short two hundred sixty bucks, and I told him it was for back child support. Then he asked me if his ex-wife called. I said no. Then he told me to go 'f' myself and left."

"Tell Marty to move a slug into Bain's station right away. I don't want him working here. And let Security know Bain's not permitted on this property."

Slow Down ... There's Plenty of Time

THE NEXT DAY, Saturday morning, the weather dropped to a ball-freezing sixteen degrees with winds gusting up to thirty miles per hour. Gray drove his dad to their bank in order to deposit his paycheck, and Danny wanted to get some cash before having breakfast at a diner on Leavenworth. They parked outside the bank's Douglas Street entrance and walked in together.

Inside the bank's spacious lobby, Danny handed Gray his ATM card to "swipe" some cash from the teller. "Get me a hundred bucks. You remember my PIN?"

"Yeah," Gray said as he walked toward the teller line.

Danny seated himself in a lobby chair and could see a

muted flat screen TV mounted on the wall. A local "BREAKING NEWS" story got his attention and pulled him out of his chair and up to the screen. On the screen were police cars with flashers on, parked sideways on a residential street blocking all traffic. The camera zoomed in on a small house with the caption scrolling at the bottom of the screen: "Hostage situation in progress in Council Bluffs."

Instantly Danny thought of Renee, her estranged ex-husband, and the two girls. *Could it be them?* he wondered. *If it is … this is my fault.*

There was no volume coming from the screen as a foggy-breathed reporter talked into a handheld microphone a ways from the cordoned-off area.

Danny saw Gray approaching him and knew he had his smart phone with him—as always. "Get me the phone number to the Grand Avenue Café in C.B.," he said to Gray without taking his eyes off the screen.

Gray looked at his dad and then at the flat screen, and yet found and dialed the number about as fast as his dad could get his cell phone out of his coat pocket. He handed his phone to his dad, then tried to figure out what was going on.

"Is Renee there?" Danny asked the woman who answered the café phone.

Danny's fears were realized when she said, "Renee is in a terrible situation now. She's not here, sir."

Danny explained, "I was afraid of that. Her ex-husband, Darin, works for me, and I'm afraid he's the instigator of Renee's 'terrible situation.' Can you please give me Renee's address?"

"Just a minute, sir," she answered.

In about a half a minute, another woman came on the phone and gave him Renee's address along with directions to get to her house. She also gave him Renee's cell phone number.

"Thanks for that," he told her.

Danny walked over to Gray and handed his phone back to him. "Now get me Darin Bain's cell phone number from the files in Personnel, and give me the keys. I'm drivin'," Danny said as they exited the bank.

"What happened?' Gray asked.

"That nut case is holding his ex-wife hostage over the wages I garnished."

For a split second Gray saw his father relax, practicing what he'd always seen him preach in seminars in a hundred cities.

The drive to Council Bluffs was incredibly slow, considering the urgency of the situation. As Danny drove up the lift of the viaduct that crossed the Missouri River into Iowa, Gray could see that his dad was consciously slowing his speed to relax his mind—a trick he used in order to allow his mind to show him what was the best creative response to this situation.

"I got Bain's cell number," Gray said, obviously in the middle of an adrenaline rush.

"Call it, but use my phone," Danny said, handing Gray his cell phone. He continued to cruise the speed limit down Broadway. "He'll recognize the last four digits of my number 7-5-8-4."

"The numbers for 'SLUG'."

"Right."

Now Gray could see why all these companies paid his father so much money for his seminars he called "Slow down … there's plenty of time." His face was clearly relaxed, and his soft left hand was lightly holding the bottom of his steering wheel, as if he were running a simple errand. *God, this would almost be laughable … if it weren't so serious,* Gray thought after dialing Bain's cell number and handing his dad his phone.

"Odds are he won't answer," Danny predicted. "Because I surprised him. He knows it's me … and that's good."

There was no voice mail recording, but the old pro slug informed his son, "He answered and clicked off his phone. See … Bain's ex-wife thinks he's bipolar. His mind is paranoid now. He's sick and enraged because he knows I found out he made calls to Washington. And he knows I retaliated against him by taking the child support out of his check. Then I'm sure he went to Renee and either threatened to beat her or actually beat her until she told him whether or not she had any contact with me. When he realized I beat him at his own game and he couldn't get even with me, he decided to take it out on Renee. He's a sick man."

"So, he's mad at you?" Gray tried to ask calmly as they made a turn off Broadway and were closing in on the hostage situation that was now headline news.

"Yeah. And I certainly bear some of the responsibility for what's happening now. I didn't handle it properly. Like Darin, I let my anger get the better of me, and I retaliated against him instead of calmly confronting him and talking it out. Now I need to make it right … both for his sake and

Renee's." Danny changed the subject, sensing his son's anxiety. "What are you feeling right now?"

"Well … my mouth is dry. And I kinda feel like I did when you pulled me out of school. I was surprised and not sure about what was coming after cleaning out my locker."

"Uh-huh … And what have I always told you about uncertain times like this?"

"You must teach your mind to keep your body calm and as relaxed as possible. That every negative thing can be corrected by positive action and words … words traveling at the speed of sound. There's no need to rush into the herd and join them. Slow down … there's plenty of time."

"Very good," his father was pleased.

Up ahead Danny and Gray could see nearly a half-dozen Council Bluffs police cars with flashers on and several police officers making sure nobody was in harm's way of this possibly dangerous hostage situation. Danny parked behind a TV station's van that belonged to News 6, a negative omen to Gray since he'd heard that the number six was an evil number. They saw a bearded cameraman with a ponytail outside the van's open side door with his hand cupped over a cigarette trying to light it.

"You want me to stay in the car?" he asked his father, reminding Danny of the little boy with the gray eyes waiting for his dad's command whenever there was uncertainty.

Danny knew his boy would be safe near the television van and told him, "No, I want you to be the messenger."

"What do you mean?"

"I want you to tell the media I'm here to get one of my

slugs back. And that everything will work out if we slow things down and relax. Bain might be watching … so keep it positive."

Gray's jaw was dropped as far as it could go; he looked like a soldier who'd just received his orders from a crazy man who was telling him to do something equally crazy.

"Bain is egotistical enough that I'm betting he's watching this play out on TV. So let him know I'm here. Can you do that?"

"What are you gonna do, Dad?"

Danny turned off his car's engine and handed his son the keys. "I don't know. Something," he shrugged and smiled while getting out of the car and dialing Bain's phone number again.

Gray watched his dad holding his cell phone to his ear as his dad walked toward the flashing police cars blocking off any traffic on the residential street where Renee and her daughters lived. He and his father could see several spooked, curious neighbors watching the scene unfold as they peered through their living room windows. They seemed to be waiting for something to happen so they could return to the normalcy of their dull lives.

Bain still wasn't answering his phone as Danny approached some police officers. To the police he appeared like a successful businessman in his full-length black cashmere coat with matching scarf, black leather gloves, and black wool cap covering his ears. "Officers, my name is Danny Mack. Darin Bain, the man holding his ex-wife hostage, works for me. I know I can help if I can talk to him."

Right away one of the officers got on his phone in his

cruiser to relay Mr. Mack's information to his superiors positioned behind the SWAT team vehicle parked in front of Renee's mother's little house.

Meanwhile, back at the News 6 van Gray pointed toward the businessman talking to the police and said to the cameraman, "If I were you, I'd keep my camera on that man in the black coat over there."

"Yeah? Why's that?" the man droned apathetically.

"Because he's my dad ... the King of Slugs."

"King of Slugs? What's that?"

"Somebody living under great stress."

"That's pretty much everybody," the bearded cameraman chuckled.

"Exactly. My dad can correct most negative things."

"How?"

"By just talking about it."

"Oh, really?" the man played along with the wacko kid with the nerd glasses. But he nonchalantly grabbed his shoulder-mounted digital camera and focused it on Danny, if only because he didn't want to miss something big if this King of Slugs guy was going to do something.

Danny walked past the police barricades toward Renee's house. As he approached the front porch steps, a cop wearing a bullet-proof vest shouted into his bullhorn, "YOU IN THE BLACK COAT! STOP AND TURN AROUND NOW!"

But Danny kept walking, calmly climbing the front porch steps of Renee's mother's house.

"SIR! THIS IS AN ORDER! STOP!"

Danny ignored the police and dialed Bain's cell phone again, betting this time he'd answer while he was on the front porch.

Darin Bain watched his ex-boss standing on his ex-mother-in-law's front porch on TV as his cell phone rang again. Bain's voice on his cell phone was angry because of the cops surrounding him, "What do YOU want?"

"I want you to help me get this gun-control issue handled," Danny said into his cell phone while standing on the front porch.

"You GOT to be kidding," Bain scoffed. "You give my ex two hundred sixty outta my check because you found out I made those calls! And now you want MY help? 'F' YOU!"

"If you hurt anybody … you are one sick coward, Darin Bain. And I swear I WILL start calling politicians again Monday morning, and we'll use your name in every call we make. You really think you should have a gun right now?"

"'F' YOU!" he screamed again, loud enough that Danny could hear him both on the phone and through the front door.

"I'll make you an offer, Darin. You come out now without harming anybody, and I'll guarantee you will help others like you who don't want to live this way."

"What's that 'f'-ing mean?"

"It means that cops and courts and lawyers can't help you. It means I'll get you the professional help you need in order to live well. I know about sick guys like you who are too ashamed and full of your worthless pride to get any help."

"How do you know anything?"

"You're the big boy with the gun. Open your door and let me in." Danny ended the call by closing his cell phone, then he stepped up close to the front door knowing the SWAT team was ready to take a shot. Danny turned around with his hands raised and called out to the police, "DON'T SHOOT! HE'S LETTING ME IN! RELAX!"

Danny heard the front door unlocking.

At the News 6 van the cameraman had zoomed in on Danny's back when he entered the house and the door closed right away behind him. Gray's excited words could be heard off camera, "He's in! Everything's okay! My dad will take over now!"

Danny lowered his arms upon seeing Renee sitting submissively on the couch with a swollen face after the beating Darin gave her. "Where are your daughters?" Danny asked Bain, who now look frazzled and was pointing the handgun with shaking hands at his ex-boss.

"I sent 'em away with Renee's ma. The old bat called the cops as soon as she got away from the house." Darin's shoulders twitched and his head jerked to one side, appearing to Danny as if he was on a manic high.

"Is that why you hit Renee? Or was there some other reason?"

"'F' YOU, Danny Mack … the King of Quacks!" Bain laughed, which made Danny laugh too.

"Darin, I can't believe you're doing this because of the money I took out of your check and gave to Renee. You are one sick cat, Darin Bain. And you're holding a gun. My best friend was bipolar like his dad. He was young … about your age … and he had a gun too. He thought he'd self-medicate by reading the Bible and praying for help … until one day he used his gun on himself. But I don't think you're like him in that way. You wouldn't pray or kill yourself … unless you killed someone else first. You wouldn't want somebody else to punish you. You're too selfish for that."

"'F' you, Mack!"

"Let's talk about what I know about Darin Bain. You're a good slug with good numbers … better than average. And you've proven to me that I was foolish for calling Washington for *gun* control. We need *people* control … background checks for people like you who are angry … bipolar … whatever. Do you really think you should have access to a gun, Darin, when two hundred and sixty bucks can set you off like this? I see clearly now how people like you need professional, sustained help … or bad things can happen. But you have to be able to see that and want the help, or it doesn't matter. So let's get down to the business of what I can do for Darin Bain. My attorney is waiting for my call that will get you real help for your chemical imbalance … as long as you don't hurt anybody. I'll get Renee to not press assault charges. And when your self-centered, negative mind is healed … I want you to help save some of those eighteen thousand slugs every year who kill themselves. And you can help them, Darin Bain."

Danny could see that he had reached his slug.

"I'm sorry I went behind your back and took money out of your check for Renee. I wanted revenge for you going behind *my* back and calling politicians with your own message that negated all of our calls. I was pissed and

… well, you know about revenge. Renee … you won't say a word about any of this to anyone but my attorney. And tell your girls the same thing … okay?"

Renee gave a positive nod.

Danny continued, "Darin, give me the bullets in your gun. I'll put 'em in my sock and I'll throw the gun on the porch." Danny extended his open hand. "An unloaded gun found by the police and reported by the media will help you. I'll tell the cops you're unarmed and comin' out with your hands raised, and nobody's been hurt."

Danny couldn't be sure what Darin was thinking right then, but he removed the ammo clip, took out all the rounds, handed them to Danny, and put the empty clip back in the gun before handing the gun over to his ex-boss. Danny dropped the ammo into one of his socks and told his slug, "Okay. Good job, Darin. I'm going to open the door and throw the gun out on the lawn. I'll tell the police that you're coming out unarmed. Just keep your hands raised and hit the deck when you go out onto the porch. Renee, you stay right behind me, and don't say anything to the police or the media."

She nodded yes again.

Danny opened the front door, tossed the gun past the porch and onto the lawn, and called out to the police that they were all coming out. Renee stepped outside right behind Danny onto the front porch. "EVERYONE IS SAFE!" Danny barked.

On the little TV screen mounted on the digital shoulder-mounted camera, Gray saw his dad and Renee on the porch with Darin face-down on the porch with his hands clasped behind his head. The SWAT team moved in, handcuffed Bain, and pulled him to his feet.

The camera showed Bain escorted into a police vehicle, then followed it as it left the scene with its lights flashing and siren wailing. Danny and Renee were escorted to separate police cars as police swarmed inside the house. It was over.

Gray was relieved and happy that his dad had defused a dangerous situation without an awful outcome. That's when a News 6 reporter came over to Gray and asked him on camera, "Was that your father who rescued that woman?"

"Yes. He's Danny Mack, the King of Slugs. He slows things down and people relax."

When Danny was being driven to the police station, he asked a policeman if he could use his cell phone to call his son and his lawyer. He called Gray and gave him relayed directions to the station. Then he told Gray he had to go because his lawyer was calling after seeing him on TV.

Bob Jensen, Danny's friend and lawyer, was a big man in physical stature. He was at the station to see his client within ten minutes of Danny arriving at the station. Both Renee and Danny refused to talk to the police until Jensen was present.

Gray was sitting in a waiting area at the police station when Jensen arrived. Jensen wanted Gray to come with him while he conferred with his dad and Renee.

In a private conference room with all three of his clients together, Jensen asked Gray why he was on TV talking about his father.

Danny answered for his son, "I wanted Gray to be the

messenger. If Darin Bain was watching, I wanted him to see that I was there to help erase the mistake I made. I knew he would let me inside when he knew I was there. The media and police would only create drama and fear, and that would work against a positive resolution. For some reason there's a concerted effort to keep Americans herded by fear. It's a real problem that's ignored by the media … because they profit from fear and more often than not just contribute to the problem."

Jensen only took one deep breath, knowing his client well enough to say with a grin, "I had to ask."

Renee Bain didn't say anything incriminating the entire time she was in the police station. Jensen informed the police that she did not want to press charges against her ex-husband. And considering that the gun wasn't loaded, Darin Bain would only be charged with aggravated assault.

Jensen was allowed to visit with his client Darin Bain in a holding cell to deliver more good news. "Mr. Mack has agreed to pay your five thousand dollar bail *if* you agree to see a doctor for your bipolar condition. And you can live in one of his apartments in the Butter Roast Building next to Telemaster and continue working at Telemaster as long as you pay all your child support to Renee on time every month. *If* you agree to these terms, Renee will not press any charges. Do you understand?"

Darin, his eyes tired-red from the stress he caused, nodded and muttered, "Yes." He was too ashamed to look anywhere but the holding cell's floor.

As the friend and lawyer of Danny turned to walk away, Bain called out to him, "Hey … why's he doing this?"

Jensen lumbered his six-foot-four-inch, 280-pound frame back to his new client and forced a courtesy smile when he said, "He's turning a negative situation into a positive one. That's what he does. He's the King of Slugs."

Gray drove Renee back to her house while his dad rode in the back with her and explained, "I really believe Darin can turn his life around after getting the right meds to even him out."

"He's angry about being sick in his brain. He says being bipolar is a sign of weakness … that he'd rather be dead than have a mental illness. He won't go to a doctor. He's got a big issue with doctors and the drugs they prescribe," Renee sighed with weary resignation after the day's ordeal.

"He's never been diagnosed as bipolar by a doctor?"

She shook her head no.

"Then how does he know he's bipolar?"

"His dad's bipolar. Now his dad takes meds and does well. But Darin doesn't want to be like his dad at all. He hates him and sees him as weak."

Nearing Renee's house, Danny asked her if she thought Darin would follow through and take him up on his offer to keep his job, live in his building, and get professional help.

"I'm not tryin' to be negative, but I think he'll leave town and start over and forget about here … especially payin' me child support. But maybe I'm wrong. I believe in miracles. I mean, look how you helped him already get out of jail and who knows what else?"

Danny walked Renee up the front porch steps. As soon as they reached the front door, her two girls ran outside onto the cold porch and greeted her in tears, relieved to see that their mother was safe.

"Thanks for everything, Mr. Mack," Renee said with an arm around each of her daughters. She waved goodbye from her front door.

Danny waved back, smiling as he headed to his car.

As Gray drove them home Danny proclaimed, "This experience with Bain has shown me clearly that unstable minds must not have access to firearms when anger can lead to violence."

"Guns are just too big a part of what our society is," Gray said. "Look at the movies where a so-called 'action hero' gets revenge by killing his enemies. Glorified wars, violent video games … Just like at Midtown High, in San Diego kids brought guns to school just to show them off. It didn't matter that they weren't loaded. They just thought it was cool to have a gun."

Gray watched his dad remove a shoe and reach down into his sock to retrieve the bullets from Bain's gun. "I told Bain to give me these to reduce his chances of going to prison."

"So his gun was loaded?"

Danny showed Gray the ammo in his hand.

"Wow! I'm just glad he gave 'em to ya."

"Me too. I wasn't sure he would."

After a moment of silence Gray confessed, "Dad, I kinda got carried away on TV."

"How so?"

"I said how you would make a great president because

you know how to get problems handled … by slowing things down … and how that's what America needs more than ever."

"You said that?" his father was shocked.

"Yeah … and I said a lot more stuff."

"Such as?"

"Like how in Al Gore's book *The Future,* he wrote about entropy and how eventually everything breaks down when isolated. That's what our country is doing. It's breaking down because we are all isolated slugs paying our bills, and we're on this treadmill of habits just to survive. And I said if we don't become united against entropy with ever-growing involvement, the planet will remain terminally ill and will not sustain us."

"Wow! You said all that?"

"Yeah. I got it from you and Al."

"So what does that have to do with me running for president?" he asked his driver. Then he added, "Get over in the right lane so I can toss Bain's ammo into the river."

"Remember when I did that essay in English class that you helped me with?"

"Yeah," Danny smiled when recalling the good ideas he'd given Gray for his assignment "If I Were President."

"I got an 'A' and Mr. Hayes had me stand up in class and read it. Well, I titled the essay "Be the Messenger" and listed the ideas you gave me that any responsible, civic-minded presidents should have. You said how our current president represents one of two parties in a system that no longer serves working people. I wrote down everything you said word for word. Most of the guys didn't like the 'slower pace' stuff by dropping the national speed limit."

"Did you explain *why* we need a fifty-five-mile-per-hour limit?"

"Yep. I said when Nixon reduced the limit to fifty-five in the seventies during the gas shortages, traffic accidents and injuries and deaths were reduced on the nation's roads to such a degree that more lives were saved on our nation's highways during that period than all the American servicemen deaths in Viet Nam that occurred while Nixon was president."

"It's true!" Danny declared as they parked and walked to their apartment building's elevator.

"Yeah, but most of the kids in school are hooked on speed … doing things fast. They don't care if lives are saved by slowing down."

"Uh-huh. But what do you expect when kids have been raised on fast food, video games, action movies, and the internet?"

When entering their apartment Danny said, "Then why would I run for president on a campaign to slow things down when most of the younger voters wouldn't vote for my ideas?"

"I think you're wrong, Dad. Like you said, 'Be the messenger.' I could be your campaign manager and see just how many votes we could get from the kids today who will be old enough to vote in 2016. There're millions of us who are young now who would welcome a slower pace and a more relaxed country. Why don't you at least see what I can do?"

"I don't know … You haven't taken the rest of your GED tests …"

"I will! I'll take 'em and get that damn diploma!"

Danny turned on the TV to the local news with his remote from his recliner. Right away he saw his face on the screen with the words below his picture, "Danny Mack, Owner of Telemaster of Omaha." Camera footage from earlier showed Danny entering Renee's house alone during the hostage situation. The next thing they showed was Gray being interviewed by the cameraman.

"So that was your father who just went inside that house, and you're not concerned because he's this 'King of Slugs?' What does that mean?"

"'Slugs' is an acronym for 'somebody living under great stress,' and my dad has called himself that since before I was born. He does things slow. And he gets things done by having people relax and do positive things."

"And so he went into that house because an employee of his is inside that house holding his ex-wife hostage?"

"Right. The man is one of my dad's slugs. They will resolve this peacefully. The police should know this. That's the message I want the police to know … to relax and slow down … because the King of Slugs is here."

The screen then flashed to the scene of Bain surrendering on the porch. Gray's off-screen words played over the video, "See, that's my dad … the best man to be the next president in four years."

Danny muted the TV.

Gray reminded his dad, "You said 'be the messenger,'"

Gray's puckish smile made Danny laugh. "Hey, it's your turn to make dinner," Danny reminded Gray, pointing to the kitchen.

"Dad, can I ask you a personal question?"

"Sure," he said as he put down Al Gore's book *The Future,* which he was reading for the second time.

"How come you haven't had a girlfriend since Mom?"

"Ya know … I asked myself that question. And all I came up with is my work … Telemaster."

"But Dad, you're rich, smart and funny. I don't get it."

"I've met women here and there, but I never wanted to mix them with my work. The truth is, I don't do intimacy well. Even when I was married to your mom, I knew I had to get my business life going. Now, it's just not important to me. Seems like the longer you go without a relationship … the easier it gets."

"So, you're afraid you'll make a mistake again?"

"That wasn't a mistake … because we got you."

"I think you're afraid to get hurt."

"Well, yeah, that too," Danny confessed, and they both laughed. "Now go make us something to eat," he pleaded, then picked up his book and began reading.

Celebrity Slugs

MONDAY MORNING, DANNY and Gray walked to work following Tenth Street to their shortcut path along the viaduct that led to the front entrance of the main building of Telemaster, which Danny referred to as TM North. Danny had called Marv earlier that morning to advise him that Darin Bain would be permitted to return to work. The two pedestrians spotted trouble when they reached Eleventh Street in front of the main entrance. Several media vehicles, including News 6, were parked in the spaces reserved for visitors of Telemaster.

Gray saw the same cameraman from News 6 who had interviewed him Saturday morning. He was having a smoke while leaning against his vehicle.

"Let me do the talking," Danny said discreetly to Gray

as they approached the dock to Telemaster.

The media converged on father and son, asking questions with cameras and microphones pointed at them as they continued walking. "Mr. Mack ... Can we ask you to comment on Saturday's hostage situation?"

"There was no big, dangerous hostage situation. The gun wasn't loaded, so there's no story here," Danny stated as they continued toward the main entrance. They walked right past the barrage of questions.

Inside peaceful Telemaster, Marv Lewis and another security guard were keeping reporters out. Marv told his boss, "Good morning, Mr. Danny. Mr. Bain is waiting for you by his cube."

"That's great news, Marv," Danny said with a broad grin. "I'll go talk to him right away."

Slug Central was humming with slugs calling all over the country. Danny sent Gray off to get started on projects while he headed for Bain's cube. He could feel every pair of eyes in the building on him. Danny stayed conscious of the fact that it took incredible courage for Bain to come back to Telemaster. And if Darin Bain wanted help, he came to the right place.

Bain was standing outside his cube because a new slug was seated at his workstation and was being trained by the senior slug in the same cube. Darin was dressed in a worn black wool sports jacket and jeans. It was as if he were about to interview for a job. His countenance looked like a poster ad for a shamed man with bipolar mental illness who was ready for help. He shook Danny's hand right away.

"I'm so happy you're here, Darin. Did the media

hounds come after ya?"

"No, they didn't recognize me. I kept my face hidden."

"Good." Danny, a pro at getting people to relax around him, leaned against one of the clear cube partitions.

Bain said, "I called Renee and the girls and her mom to apologize to them. I told them I was getting help for my bipolar and that I'm going to pay my child support on time. If you were serious about giving me my job back, I'm going to talk to Payroll at the end of my shift today and tell them to make the deduction from my check and send it directly to her."

Danny kept still, smiling and nodding positively upon hearing Darin's incredibly good news. "How are you feeling now?" Danny asked his slug.

"I was up all night in one of those manic highs I've been getting. I'm comin' down now."

"Uh-huh. You want to work and live here?"

"Oh, yes, Mr. Mack. I want to get help for my bipolar and live here. Keepin' my job is a big part of that. I like workin' here … and I'm sorry for makin' those calls. I had no right to do that."

"Good. Well … we're starting new and turning things to a positive. I want us to keep headed in that direction … where you can manage your health situation and live well. Okay?"

"Okay," Darin nodded humbly with his head bent in contrition.

"Do you have healthcare with us?" Danny asked.

"No," he shook his head.

"I'm going to HR right now and let them know you're still working for us … as if nothing happened. And I'm going to have Helen, our Health Services manager, stop by your cube and give you the phone numbers to doctors near us who can help you. I'll have the doctor's office bill Telemaster directly for any care you get related to your bipolar. Schedule your appointments after your shift. I'll have Marv, our housing manager in Butter Roast, show you your studio after your shift. Okay?"

Darin was choked up with gratitude to get this kind of second chance. "Thank you, Mr. Mack," he said as he extended his right hand.

"You're welcome."

"Can I start calling now?"

Danny went over to the new slug in Bain's chair and told him to move to the other station in the cube to continue his training. Then Danny told the other slug in the shared workstation that Darin would be training the new slug, and to go see the floor manager to be assigned to another workstation.

Soon the rehired slug donned his headset at his workstation and began calling for his client. "Hi! This is Darin with Midwest Chiropractic on Jones Street! We're calling our business neighbors …"

Danny walked away feeling elated that Darin was animated and on his way to a new life. Other slugs in nearby cubes could see that Darin was back with the Telemaster family.

Danny didn't advertise what he did for Darin Bain. He didn't have to. His slugs did it for him. Yet not one slug at Telemaster talked to the media that day. No memo needed to be posted. They all knew that their leader wasn't about to get involved in a question-and-answer session that involved one of his slugs who was hurting now.

Later that same day Danny had his housing manager, Marv, meet Darin at the end of his shift to show him his new studio apartment next door. The affable retired Navy man escorted Darin to the fourth floor skywalk that connected the two buildings. That way Darin was able to avoid any lurking vultures wanting an interview with the mystery man who surrendered to police in the hostage situation.

Darin liked his furnished studio with full bath and moved in right away. He slept twelve hours straight that first night, knowing he was going to see a doctor after his shift the next afternoon.

The media kept trying to contact Danny about the hostage situation, but Shelly deflected every call with the words her boss told her to say, "Neither Mr. Mack nor his employees are interested in becoming celebrity slugs."

*   *   *

Just as every hot local story cools down in a few days, this one did too. The following weekend brought a foot of snow to Omaha, and reporters lost interest in the King of Slugs.

Gray and his dad finished the February *Peaceful Trails* newsletter and sent it to over ten thousand slugs on the internet after Shelly edited it. Even though the hostage incident was not mentioned, members by the thousands sent feedback regarding Danny's list of campaign promises the next president should make in a country caught up in the business of bottom lines. The King of

Slugs' mantra—Slow down ... there's plenty of time—had gone viral since the incident in Council Bluffs.

Apparently, Telemaster and other local viewing slugs had spread the story about Danny Mack to other slugs around the country. Ninety thousand new members joined *Peaceful Trails* within twenty-four hours after Danny announced in the February newsletter there would be no more membership fees. From now on it was free, and that caused an incredible surge of slugs to join.

One morning at work Gray was talking to his dad while his dad was hanging upside down on the inversion table. They were discussing the increase in new members. Gray was letting his dad know that many of the new members were teens from fourteen to nineteen years old. "And more than half are boys! Dad, you know what most of them are saying about you?"

"What?" Danny was curious while taking the compression off his back.

Gray sat in front of his computer screen reading aloud while scrolling through some of the emails from members. "Danny Mack for President. ... King of Slugs for President. ... What a campaign trail! ... Run in 2016. ... King of Slugs has my vote. ... YES! A massive prison in Alaska for cowards who use a gun to commit a crime. Just what this country needs! ... Tougher laws and mental health funding for our sick country. ... Go Danny Go! ... Agreed! We need to speed up the post office. Everyone wants their checks faster. ... Referendum voting is a must. ... We need a Slug Central, not a White House!"

Gray got up from his chair and went over to his dad. He looked down at his upside-down face and said, "Dad, I swear … what you were saying about an independent candidate winning the presidency and how that's the *one thing* that's going to shake up these partisan politicians to do what the people want … the people agree. Like this one …" Gray went back to his computer screen and scrolled until he found the right email to read out loud, "Our parents and grandparents are too entrenched in their politics to change, and we want a country that works for US slugs. Special interest groups, corporations, and the elite are not who we are! A democracy means the majority rules, and slugs are the majority, aren't we? We need some justice for the majority and someone has to lead us! Let it be the King of Slugs!"

Gray went back to the inversion table where his dad was upright and getting out of the ankle supports and back onto his feet. "Dad, these emails are from all kinds of slugs! They're students and working people who want *you* to run for president! And if you do run, I'll be your campaign manager because I can reach millions of young people like me who want change now. They don't want to pay the debts of their parents and grandparents while corporations pay ZERO taxes. They want to know someone is working for them who will make this a better country!"

"When's your next GED test?" Danny asked.

"Tomorrow."

"Tomorrow," his dad repeated, his ego still thinking about running for president. Then he surprised Gray when he told him, "If I'm going to run as an independent, there will be no TV ads, no sound bites, and no hidden agendas."

"Right. Just the internet," Gray agreed.

"I'm not a liberal or a conservative … to the left or right of center. I'm an independent who would run for real change without taking one dime from any corporations or special interest groups."

"Right. You'd only take contributions from other slugs."

"Precisely," Danny agreed absently while looking through the mint-green glass walls of his office at the maze of workstations. Then he said, "Everything will be transparent … on the table. No backroom deals made with any block of voters or to satisfy any egos of politicians."

"Right."

"But I can't have a campaign manager who isn't at least a high school graduate," he turned his gray eyes on his son and smiled.

"Tomorrow … I take another test tomorrow," Gray assured him, returning his smile.

"Good. You get your diploma and I'll consider it."

"You will?" Gray was elated.

"Why not? If the media's right, I wouldn't stand a chance because I wouldn't spend the millions of dollars on ads with those shysters. Another thing … no major network interviews. Only Charlie Rose and Bill Moyers. I like Charlie and Bill. They won't dig for negatives."

"Dad, it's like you say, 'When a slug's trailing … he's on the move.'"

Danny laughed and said, "That's so cool. Make a note of that for the campaign."

Gray went back to his computer's screen, and his father joined him to look at some more feedback from slugs that the February newsletter generated.

So Many Slugs

DAY AFTER DAY new slugs continued logging on to the *Peaceful Trails* website. Mostly teens and young adults in their twenties were joining the free newsletter to read Danny Mack's seven campaign proposals he would make *if* he ran for president:

1. Reduce the national debt by reducing defense spending by ten percent every year.
2. Consistent referendum national voting on important issues to get slugs working together for better government.
3. Make a consistent effort to make it a federal offense to commit a crime using a firearm.

4. Make a consistent effort to build a massive penitentiary in Alaska that would house and rehabilitate felons who commit a crime with a firearm. This place would be known as Zero Tolerance. "One strike, you're in."
5. Massive funding for sick people with a mental illness.
6. Get the United States Postal Service to show a profit within two years.
7. Conserve energy and slow the pace of our country by reducing the nation's speed limit to fifty-five miles per hour on all our highways.

In the newsletter, Danny said that each one of these seven proposals would be voted on by the nation so that elected representatives passed legislation willed by the majority. He also asked all members to list these promises in their order of importance, along with other issues that interested them. He also stated that feedback on any of the seven proposals that were not of interest—and why—would be appreciated.

*　　*　　*

By the time February was over, Gray had taken and passed all of his GED tests and was now free to devote all of his creative energies to his work at Telemaster and his father's growing *Peaceful Trails* membership.

Danny wouldn't commit to running for the nation's

highest office because he was not sure if he was up to the task of responding to the enormous entitlements his generation of baby boomers was going to demand regarding healthcare and Social Security. His plan of attack on these pressing entitlement issues was inchoate. He one time remarked to Gray, "I don't like the way the current president doesn't seem to be pressing for action to begin the painful raising of revenue for these baby boomers. He may be winding us down from two wars, but too many slugs have stated that they don't want our money going to rebuild and stabilize Iraq and Afghanistan when we can't even pay our retired seniors without backroom politics and last-minute deals with all these partisan lawyers and their egos who don't ever hesitate to vote themselves a cost-of-living increase."

Meanwhile, his eighteen-year-old campaign manager was analyzing and providing incredible data from members to his busier-than-ever boss.

One day in early March, Gray showed his father the graphic design he'd been working on since even before the hostage incident. It made an immediate positive impression with his father and made him want to do something about what he called "the mess we all created."

"I want to put it on the March newsletter," Gray stated.

Danny stood over him looking down at his computer screen at a large green snail with a crown on its head. An American flag waved from one of its antennae as Gray rode on its back while holding his open laptop and wearing his headphones. There was a trail of green snail slime with words "Slow down … there's plenty of time."

The Washington D.C. cityscape was drawn on the horizon, and they appear to be headed in that direction. Gray played one of Danny's favorite meditation songs, "Looking Glass" by Northcore. The snail on the graphic appeared to be moving on the computer screen to the music.

"I like that," Danny was pleased. "It's a positive, forward-moving, upbeat song." Changing the subject Danny asked Gray, "How many members do we have now?"

"About two hundred and twenty thousand," Gray answered.

"How many are eighteen and older?" Danny asked.

Gray started typing on his keyboard. "Sixty-two thousand, eight hundred and twenty."

"So a little less than a hundred and sixteen thousand are under eighteen?"

"Right," Gray agreed.

"I want you to find out from a Slug Alert how many of those eighteen and over would register as an independent voter. And how many of them already registered as a Democrat or Republican would vote for an independent candidate for president."

Gray's eyes widened with excitement, but his father stopped his rising enthusiasm by saying, "The numbers have to be credible, Gray. This isn't American Idol. This is as big as it gets, and I'm *not* going to consider running for *any* office until I know at the very least that slugs would register as an independent ... and without media attention. I refuse to raise money for TV ads that entrenched senior voters with tunnel vision watch ... voters who believe what they hear on TV and vote for their party regardless of the issues at stake and the hidden agendas lobbyists of the elite and corporations support. I refuse to ask for campaign funds from my slugs to throw away on the few media moguls who decide which pundits get their air time."

"I get it, Dad. You want to start something on the internet without asking slugs for campaign money to run TV ads. Let's just see what we can do," Gray said calmly with a steadfast serenity that his father felt and admired right away.

Danny knew that when he was Gray's age, he didn't have a clue about anything except fear and poverty. It was liberating to see his independent-thinking, proactive son so eager to do something to change the course of the country's history. "Find out the rules or laws that an independent candidate has to meet in order to run for president," he told his campaign manager. "I'm sure there's some kind of bottleneck baloney we'll have to comply with.

Later that same day, Danny told Burt to look into what expenses can be deducted during a campaign.

"What kind of campaign?" his accountant had to know.

"I'm considering running for president as an independent."

Since Burt was also his friend he could ask, "Are you kidding me?"

"It's just an idea I'm kicking around. I'm still researching the numbers and red tape."

"You'll need a campaign manager," Burt replied, obviously insinuating himself.

"I have one. Gray."

"Gray?" his friend looked even more incredulous as Gray worked at his desk.

Before Burt left his office, Danny told him to keep the news to himself—except for Shelly, of course—until he announced it to his slugs. Danny then leaned back in his swivel chair with his hands clasped behind his head and watched Gray search the internet for information.

Danny's thoughts switched to Darin Bain, and he asked Shelly on his phone intercom to come to his office. She did, her mind still focused on her husband discreetly telling her about Danny's political plan.

"Find out how Darin Bain is doing," Danny instructed her. "Get his appointment stats. Check with Marv and find out how he's doing in his studio. And check with Payroll to see if he followed through on the paycheck deductions to make his child support."

Within the hour Danny heard good news. Marv said that Bain was a good tenant. Bain's set appointments were up an amazing twenty percent in the last month, and Payroll said he was paying his child support by automatic bank deposits every payday into Renee's account. Upon hearing this good news, the boss timed a visit to Darin's cube right at the end of his shift. Right off he could see that his slug looked healthier, and he asked Darin, "So have you gone to a doctor regarding your bipolar condition?"

Darin told his boss, "I've gone a few times, and I'm on a medication that seems to be working for me."

Leaving Bain's cube, Danny thought about how good things were turning out for his slug—all because he got involved. Darin was now a healthier slug who liked his work and was paying his child support. Danny wondered how many of his slugs were like Darin—needing just a little help in order to produce big, positive changes. And then he thought of Gray and how his incredible outgoing words on camera in Council Bluffs had generated so many new members to their newsletter. It was clear to him that he had used the tragic story in New England as an excuse to remove his son from school in order to employ his technical skills with computers at Telemaster. It was all connected to buying back more time they had lost from the divorce and all those years of separation.

Walking over to one of his east-facing windows, Danny stopped to listen to the diminishing symphony of his 1,500-plus slugs leaving their shift. The din was soon replaced by the peaceful whirring sound of eight ceiling fans circulating the air high above Slug Central, mixed with the keening wind all around his old building that portended a winter storm. *Should I do this campaign thing for Gray's future? Or because it will temporarily motivate millions of slugs out there who I know are waiting and wanting to put their energies into getting things done that are far greater than the stressful lives they endure every day? We are not our government today. We are slugs of all ages who want to be represented by other slugs.*

As the sounds of the first shift departing were replaced by the second shift arriving, Danny got in touch with the notion that he really liked his idea about running an independent campaign without TV ads and networks getting his message out there. They could dig into his past and find that he had no scandals or negative stories involving women, and there were no campaign contributors he had to please. He believed he was a credible candidate with one group of Americans who would support him: slugs—working people who were too busy on the treadmill of American life paying their bills to do anything else.

Still standing at his east-facing window, his campaign song "Looking Glass" started to play throughout Slug Central. He could see the eastern sky was about to drop that foot of snow that had been predicted by forecasters. He thought of Gray's suggestion to increase referendum voting in their newsletter because of the vast amount of information it would provide from members voting online for or against important issues.

Last night Gray had informed his dad that feedback showed a vast majority of slugs wanted more prison time for felons who commit a crime with a firearm, and that many of the members were expressing how repeat felons of gun crimes have zero respect for laws and life. They also expressed their belief that a federal prison for these gun felons in Alaska with longer prison time and structured rehabilitation would deter thousands of gun crimes.

Now, with Gray's research, Danny was aware that he would be far more successful running for the highest office instead of a senate or congressional district seat. It was more clear that the political system in America is rigged to support two mainstream parties in ninety-nine percent of the country because of gerrymandering, a political way to ensure that party candidates get elected.

Amid the rising calls of his second shift, Danny could see how a silent campaign by the silent majority of slugs could make an impact and put the powers in Washington on edge, especially if he convinced his slugs to not vote for any of the two major parties that are part of the problem. Danny liked that idea.

Campaign Trail

B Y EARLY APRIL 2013 it was unofficial. Danny Mack announced to over 300,000 members of his newsletter that he was running as an independent candidate for president, and that his eighteen-year-old son, Gray, was his campaign manager.

Right before the April newsletter came out, Gray hired a Creighton University student photographer to take his father's photograph for the upcoming newsletter. Danny wore his forest-green wool sports jacket with jeans and a black t-shirt.

It was also announced in the newsletter that Danny was currently researching whether to join the Green or Libertarian independent party in order to avoid the endless hassles of getting on the ballot in most states; the regulations for most states make it nearly impossible to start a new independent political party. Danny thought his campaign proposals leaned more toward the Green Party since his national fifty-five-mile-per-hour speed limit would conserve energy and save thousands of lives, not to mention saving hundreds of billions of dollars in damages and health costs.

Gray was spending eighteen hours a day, seven days a week, working on his father's soft campaign—proving to his father as well as himself that he was as committed as possible. At first Gray believed his dad's biggest block of potential voters in 2016 were present-day fifteen- to twenty-one-year-olds. He believed those were the flexible minds open to voting for his dad. But it was the candidate himself who thought unregistered slugs of all ages were reachable up to the point that they were too entrenched in a party. Or just too apathetic.

"We have to get them to register as independents. That's what we have to do. Reach the unregistered voters of all ages," Danny told his campaign manager. "You can't be bothering fifteen-year-olds to vote for anything in three or four years. God, when I was fifteen, I was still watching cartoons and had no concept of *next week* … let alone an election three years down the road."

*   *   *

It was amazing and wonderful and even a little humbling to Gray and Danny that Darin Bain let them know he was interested in helping out at the rally. Telemaster slugs were buzzing about the rally after it was mentioned in a Slug Alert that Danny was indeed considering running for the nation's highest office.

Darin was doing incredibly well on his medication and had transformed himself in less than ninety days. He went from an angry man with no future to a smiling cherubic face with a positive attitude that every slug noticed.

"You really runnin' for president?" Bain asked from his workstation when his boss was walking by.

"I don't know yet. It'll be more like a test-run campaign until Gray and I are sure we can help motivate unregistered slugs to register as independents. Gray's my campaign manager and video director. We're just going to have fun with it and see where it goes."

"I'll vote for ya," Darin smiled.

"Are you a registered voter?" Danny asked from the entrance to Bain's cube.

"No … but I will register if you run." Darin offered to help out in any way he could for Danny's campaign if he needed any.

"Everybody needs a little help," his boss smiled and waved to his transformed slug as he started back to his office.

*   *   *

Danny insisted they do all their early campaigning via webcam. He rationalized, "Chances are this whole thing will fizzle out and nothing will come from it."

"And no TV ads," Gray reiterated.

"Absolutely not. We're not playing that game."

It was at this time that Danny confessed to his son that his motives had been selfish when he took him out of school early like he did. "It wasn't just the New England massacre. I needed you at Telemaster for tech support to keep the business running. And I really do think this campaign thing could be that 'something crazy' we do together. I know politics are slanted against an independent even running, but these slugs keep telling us there's something there. And I think whether we ride this out or get blocked along the way, we have to let every slug know what we find out."

Gray agreed and told his dad, "I want to start directing short videos on the internet and make them fun."

"Fun is good."

"And you said you'd like to address one of your campaign proposals."

"Right."

"Which one?"

CP-1

NOT MORE THAN two blocks from Telemaster was the Omaha Postal Annex. At just the right spot on the sidewalk, Gray positioned his digital camera on a tripod and looked through his lens at his father, who was standing behind a podium that had the crowned green snail logo attached to the front of it. Danny, the presidential candidate, was humorously and obviously wearing a bullet-proof vest under his sweater. Post Office vehicles and the loading dock were visible in the background.

A gathering of spectators—twenty or so Telemaster slugs, including Burt and Shelly and Darin—were in the group to hear the candidate. The camera moved to reveal a few postal employees smoking at a table at a break area. There were a couple spectators holding signs: "Danny

Mack for Prez" and "No More Snail Mail."

The candidate appeared nervous while looking over at the postal workers before beginning his Campaign Proposal Number One, billed as CP-1. "Thanks for coming." Danny smiled into the microphone. "As you all know, I've announced my intention to run as an independent candidate for President of the United States!"

There was a timed smattering of applause from the gathering as the camera went over to the confused postal workers and back to Danny's wariness.

"The reason I'm here today is to launch my first campaign proposal to all of you slugs who will be potential voters in 2016. And I want to appeal NOW to my eighteen-year-old-and-up slugs who are already members of my newsletters—which you can find on slugcentral.com—to please register to vote as an independent. If you don't register, YOU CAN'T VOTE! And if you don't vote … well, that means that once again you haven't found a candidate worth voting for!"

He nervously cleared his throat and took a quick glance over at the postal workers on break listening to him from their break area. "My first campaign proposal is I will make the U.S. Postal Service show a profit within two years."

The crowd was still, and Danny stole another quick and wary look at the postal workers. "I will draft a bill before Congress that allows Americans to advertise on postage stamps. I'm not talking about Coca Cola's Santa, I'm talking about individual Americans who want to pay to have their face on a postage stamp. Not Elvis, not Babe Ruth, I'm talking American slugs. YOU!" he pointed to a spectator. "And YOU!" he pointed to another face in the crowd. "There are millions of slugs out there who would pay to put their mug on a stamp. Especially if it generated enough revenue to make the U.S. Postal Service solvent and show a profit *every year!*"

The applause was loud and enthusiastic.

"I know personally many slugs who would pay to put their pet on a stamp!"
More applause and a few chuckles ensued after a leashed dog in the crowd started to bark.

"The Postal Service needs a makeover! If we can't get those slugs to show a profit, how do we expect to *ever* get the deficit down?"

Danny looked over at the frowning postal workers. As soon as he turned back to his audience, an onlooker in the crowd popped a balloon, causing Danny to fearfully hit the sidewalk as if he'd been shot at during his jittery camera moment. The crowd's laughter caused Danny to get up after he realized he hadn't been shot at. He said to Gray, "We can edit that out, right?"

Danny went into the crowd to shake hands as his campaign song "Looking Glass" played. Some in the crowd began to chant "King of Slugs! King of Slugs!"

Later at night when they were at home, Gray and his dad were laughing as they watched the unedited version of CP-1 on the digital camera screen. Gray, the perfectionist director, stopped and backed up shots, all the while pointing out minor editing changes he'd make for CP-1 before putting in on the newsletter and later on YouTube.

Gray suggested, "For our next video, it would be cool

to have a Secret Service agent with suit and sunglasses in the crowd staying with the candidate as he greets the crowd.

"That's a good idea," his dad agreed. "I'm looking forward to the feedback we'll get from members after CP-1 comes out. I think they'll be entertained too."

"I was looking into some requirements for us to get on the ballot …"

"Yeah?"

"It's pretty much impossible … now."

"Yeah, but that's okay. We'll have some fun with this, Gray, and keep on slowing things down. Our newsletter is growing without advertising."

Gray went to his room, and Danny went to his recliner to read. After positioning himself back and grabbing Al Gore's book, he paused to think about how Gray had made him look "presidential" and fit in CP-1. His bright video director had darkened his skin color a shade to reduce the paleness from the Nebraska winter. And he made him sound more powerful than his usual "good-neighbor" voice, giving his words more of a commanding punch. He even made his small, flinty, gray eyes bigger and brighter with more visible color. Gray was also able to reduce his dad's flabby double chin and fat cheeks. That impressed the candidate so much that he decided to be more consistent and work out every day after lunch in the Telemaster exercise room.

Danny reflected on the day of pure creative fun he and Gray had in making CP-1.

Today was incredible, he mused. *One of our all-time best days ever! And if I hadn't taken him out of school and brought him to Telemaster, we never would have had this kind of day together."*

Upon reading a few lines from "inconvenient" Al, Danny paused to remember that moment while filming CP-1 when he was curled up on the sidewalk after that balloon popped. He had looked up at Gray and saw that beautiful laughter all over his face.

State of the Union

O N THE FIRST morning of May, Gray and his father were shocked and somewhat dubious of the fact that they were getting consistent emails from people of all ages and from all over the country saying they had registered or were going to register to vote for the first time because they wanted to vote for Danny Mack, King of Slugs.

"Thirty-one percent of our emails are from young people who will be eighteen in four years," Gray informed his dad.

Ever since CP-1 had been posted on YouTube, Shelly started fielding more and more calls from newspaper reporters and TV producers about interviewing this "King of Slugs" internet sensation.

Danny, on Gray's advice, hired a young lawyer in

Lincoln to find out exactly what each of the fifty states' requirements were to get on their ballot in 2016 as an independent candidate for the presidential election.

Meanwhile, Gray hired a team of young professionals with their own film equipment to make CP-2 while Gray and Danny developed the gist of the second campaign proposal.

The third day in May was the most perfect of days for weather: a cool sixty-six degrees with a slight breeze. It was a classic spring-fever kind of day, and Danny could sense that his first-shift slugs were anxious to get off the phone and be outside in the golden sunshine that was working hard to dry the April mud.

It was the third day in a row that Danny and Gray walked to the same Old Market restaurant just a block from work with Gray toting his expensive digital camera. Father and son, candidate and campaign manager, were about to find out if Danny Mack had the personal magnetism it took to be a viable candidate for the nation's highest office. Danny had no clue about what was going to happen soon, although he felt something would. He was certain that his quiet son, the director of his campaign videos, was setting him up for some publicity stunt to test his mettle for the coming campaign. Danny decided he didn't want to work from a script when he made CP-2, and he didn't want to know when it was to be filmed.

They walked up the clean spring sidewalk to the familiar lunch spot, and they were greeted by the same friendly host who escorted them to the same table for the third day in a row. Seated in their high-back walnut booth,

Danny opened his menu. Gray said he was going to have the hamburger deluxe.

"Three days in a row? What is this … Groundhog Day?"

"More like ground beef day," Gray said with that bespectacled poker face his dad couldn't read ever since his boy started wearing glasses.

When the same waitress came over to their table to take their order, Gray couldn't help noticing how his dad's eyes were scoping out the restaurant, looking for some "spontaneous" event that was going to happen. After ordering Danny quipped, "Good job, Mr. Campaign Director. There's not a camera in sight. And we're just having lunch together … again … right?"

Gray's positive nod was again confusing to his dad.

When their waitress brought their drinks and left again, Gray was texting on his phone. Upon finishing sending his text Danny asked, "Okay, who'd you text?"

"Indie Films. They want to know when we want to shoot CP-2."

"When *are* we shooting CP-2?" the candidate was curious.

"Sometime in early May … before the May *Peaceful Trails* comes out."

"Oh," Danny grinned, as if he were wise to the fact that he knew something was still going to happen in time to be in the newsletter that had grown to a circulation of over 600,000 readers.

After their quiet lunch, Danny paid the tab. They left the restaurant and headed back down the street toward Telemaster. Once inside Slug Central, an incredible roar rose from over three thousand slugs from both shifts. They were standing and applauding Danny as he made his way along a pathway to an elevated podium placed in front of his office area with "Looking Glass" playing over the room's sound system. A film crew was filming what resembled a State of the Union address. It was truly a surprise to the candidate as he got behind the elevated podium and adjusted the microphone. The crowd and the music were silenced after he pointed to the imaginary watch on his wrist. He then took a moment to focus on the visual reminder high above them: "Slow down … there's plenty of time."

"As most of you know, I started Telemaster alone. And then came Shelly and Burt, Marv and Jerry, Helen, and on and on. Each and every one of you slugs made us grow a little bit day by day. I think Gray was seven or eight then, weren't ya?" he asked his nodding campaign manager off to his right. "I kept seeing how each one of you were making us successful … our way."

The crowd cheered.

"Over the years of growing Telemaster, I'd get scared like all of you with kids when there was some massacre like Columbine, or even the mall mass killing here in Omaha. I'd be scared that I could lose Gray this way … and I was so far away from him the whole school year. This fear and anxiety about these kinds of insane mass shootings would come back now and then and really terrify me. And what I've been hearing from city police officers around the country is that the carnage from cowards with handguns is out of control. It's these repeat felons and cowards with guns—or ANYONE who points a weapon at a human being other than to defend themselves or loved ones—who are the cowards who have to be put away to get the real help and rehabilitation we ALL need."

Applause again rose from the crowd until he waved them down to silence.

"This is my second campaign proposal, to get two things done by a national referendum regarding crimes with firearms in our violent society. Number one will be mandating extensive background checks for ANYONE purchasing a firearm in this country!"

More applause.

"And number two will be to increase funding for mental illnesses to determine and track who has no business getting their hands on ANY firearm!"

He waved down their applause again and told his slugs, "We must have a national vote on these two points. If the votes are there, Congress has to approve the funding. I say we CAN fund these things and eliminate the billions of dollars we are sending to countries that burn our flag and want us to keep killing each other!"

The applause was incredibly loud, and Gray marveled at his dad's ability to connect with the same slugs who had voted down his rally in Washington. He scanned the four cameras positioned in Slug Central that were filming CP-2 for the internet. At the same moment his father mentioned to his slugs how he planned to avoid the mainstream media during his campaign.

"Those messengers are part of the problem! The political system is rigged to support the two political parties in control and not the REAL slugs in this country who are too busy working and paying their bills. That's ALL OF YOU!" he pointed to the faces in the crowd to more applause. "You all know that Gray is my son and campaign manager. He's a high school graduate and is good with computers. Both of us certainly have no experience in politics. But we do have one agenda: To work for America's slugs!"

The crowd again erupted in cheers and applause. Once they quieted Danny continued, "NOT Republicans … NOT Democrats … NOT the ones who vote their party line. I want the registered independent voters. I want the unregistered, apathetic slugs. And I want the vote of future slugs who will be eighteen on November 8, 2016. That's how we'll shake up this country run by corporations and the elite. And we can do it without expensive TV ads that only serve the media elite. Right now we are using our energy to get on the ballot. They don't make it easy! One more thing Gray and I want to say, because the second shift has to get to work and the first shift wants outta here … We have come to the understanding that because of our entrenched political system, right now it would be impossible for independent slugs to win a majority of seats in the House of Representatives or the Senate. That's why we've decided to go for the game winner with one long Hail Mary into the end zone! That's the only way to get these political cronies who are supported by special interests to give the people what they want. Because when we reach the top, that's the ONLY way they'll ALL know that THERE ARE MORE SLUGS THAN LOBBYISTS! Thank you for your attention and support. Now get back to work!"

The cheering died down fast because Danny hustled into his office.

Gray went into the office a few minutes later with a digital camera that he planned on using for behind-the-scenes shots and interviews for CP-2; however, the candidate was seated behind his desk with his back to Gray and the second shift settling in to work.

"That was good, Dad. ... Dad?"

Danny remained quiet while facing the stand of tall potted plants behind his desk. Gray moved around to talk to his dad, who was obviously upset about something. He waited for his dad to say something. It looked to Gray as if his father was in one of his meditative trances.

"I'm no Commander-in-Chief. Who am I kidding besides me?" he snorted a courtesy laugh. "Ten years ago I had the energy to make Telemaster grow by motivating and training my slugs out there to do things my way. Now, here we are ... this speck of dust on a polluted planet telling slugs how we're going to lock up other slugs with guns. Laws will have to be drafted and majority-approved by a bunch of lawyers who are more than part of the problem. We're a country of victims, and that's just what lawyers needed to keep us from taking action and make themselves part of the elite. Change is too painful for those slugs. Now I told 'em all I'd run as an independent ... and for *what*? So we can beat our heads against those old cronies and lawyers in Washington while entertaining a bunch of unemployed couch potatoes?" Danny looked up and into his son's steady gray eyes and said, "Maybe you should go off to college somewhere or start your own business doing something you love. I could stay at

Telemaster and be content knowing you'll have this business to fall back on someday … when I'm gone or retired."

"You're saying you want to stop the campaign?" Gray asked incredulously.

Danny looked away from him and said, "Maybe we should. Back out early … announce that we had an idea that could never get on the ballot. Like Ralph Nader. What good did he do except swing elections to one party or the other?"

"Dad, Ralph Nader had zero charisma. YOU DO!"

"Come on, Gray. Those are my employees out there! I love them and most of them at least like me. Today, the president is just a high-paid cheerleader with a nice plane."

Gray leaned down with his digital camera to show his dad a moment in CP-2 that had been recorded. "Dad, all my life you said we'd spend more time together when I turned eighteen. I turned eighteen, got out of school early to help you, and got my GED like you wanted me to. Now we have a chance to really do something incredible together besides making money and …"

Gray could now see that something else was bothering his dad. "What is it, Dad? What else about this campaign is wrong for you?"

"I'm a bachelor. How far do you think that'll go running for president? I've got intimacy issues. I've told you that. I don't trust just any woman to love me for me, now that I've put all my energy into my business."

"Dad, the majority of people are single in this country, so don't play that game. I'll bet that over half the people that ever lived in this country in the last fifty years have been divorced at least once. Stay on course with your mission to reduce gun violence in this country. Imagine what happens with tougher gun laws and thorough background checks for everybody. That's going to save some innocent lives, Dad."

Danny nodded in agreement half-heartedly.

"Even though it looks impossible to get on any state ballot unless we spend a ton of money, I thought of a good name for an independent party."

"What's that?" his dad was curious.

"U.S.ofA. United Slugs of America."

"I like it," Danny smiled.

U.S.ofA.

W ITHIN A MONTH it became clear to Danny and Gray that their unofficial campaign and newly named independent party would never begin—let alone have a trail. U.S.ofA. could never become a legitimate political party in the current American political system.

"I wouldn't even want to attempt to raise the millions of dollars it would take just to get on the ballot in a few states," Danny told his depressed campaign manager after a long consultation with a political advisor in Lincoln.

"I guess deep down I never really thought we'd even get this far," Gray admitted from his slouched seated position at his computer station in his dad's office at Telemaster.

After a bit Danny got up from his desk chair and went

over to his inversion table. He continued talking to his forlorn son while hanging upside-down. "Well, Gray … when you really stop to think about things from a different perspective, we're already running a successful campaign here with Telemaster … aren't we?"

"Yeah."

"And we're doing good work … right?"

"Right."

There was an awkward silence as Gray stared at his computer screen. All at once an idea came to him that caused him to sit up straight in his chair and swivel around to face his inverted father. "Dad, why don't we grow Telemaster into a place where high school graduates and even dropouts and homeless people can work for us and learn how to live well in this crazy country where gun violence and corporate outsourcing are just … who we have become?"

"Isn't that what we've been doing?" his dad pronounced with a nasal twang from being inverted.

"Yeah, but we've been sidetracked with getting new members and focusing on the campaign … something that's not only impossible, but you'd be resisted all the way to the White House. But here at Telemaster we can make progress in our own democracy without all that resistance."

"Yeah. Ya know, that does make sense. And you're right about how we should improve what we do here. I think we only did this campaign thing because it caught on with our subscribers. We wanted to make these big changes in Washington … but maybe we could be more proactive by focusing on how we can help slugs."

"That's exactly what I'm talking about," Gray agreed enthusiastically, "and we can still be U.S.ofA., can't we?"

"Sure we can. In fact, we can get rid of the name Telemaster and put U.S.ofA. right on our building here."

Danny was pleased that his ex-campaign manager was into the business more than ever, since he'd always wanted Telemaster to be the kind of company his son would want to work for. Maybe eventually take over.

Dropping the campaign was the end of a boy's fantasy for Gray and the closing chapter of a father's desire to make up for years of long separations from his son.

Seated across from each other at a table in the Telemaster coffeehouse and break room, Danny strategized with Gray about how their new and improved company, U.S.ofA., could help put slugs to work in a sluggish economy. "Much of the country's economic woes can be blamed on big corporations that didn't think creatively about using their assets to fund training and create new work for the American workforce."

"High school kids who aren't motivated to go to college can be as productive as anyone if given the opportunity to succeed," Gray inserted.

Danny agreed, "Most of my slugs who work here are only high school graduates. Why should kids today burden themselves with thousands of dollars of debt in order to get a slightly better salary? That same motivated worker starting at the bottom can work his or her way up with a growing company and end up in a management position … and usually be better qualified and more educated than the college graduates. I've had hundreds of my slugs over the years move on to better paying jobs. Some have even started their own businesses. My employee turnover is lower than any company I know that has mostly part-time employees. This U.S.ofA. concept could be franchised to slugs … but we would train them."

"Like an employment service."

"Yeah. But most bigger companies want to train within. We'd have to work with clients who are just starting up or small businesses wanting to grow."

"I could do all the computer graphics, design software, and we could get into all kinds of products and services that sustain the planet. Our existing model of marketing to businesses only would work for clean energy products and services …"

"I'd want to keep Telemaster going for chiropractors. It's already so well established. Why don't you put together a list of green products and services that we could market U.S.ofA. to, and start working on graphics and software to promote it. We can easily increase our calling capacity here by a third just by putting an extra phone in every cube here, with a trainer in every cube. That way an experienced slug can always be training a new slug to call for our clients with another experienced slug in the cube. Trainers can get an hourly wage increase for keeping both clients served in each cube happy."

"Dad, I could post a 'slugs wanted' ad for U.S.ofA. on our website and other employment sites where high school kids will see it. They need jobs like this whether they go to college or not."

"Yeah, that would be good. But the first thing you should do is notify all our slugs here and our newsletter subscribers that we've decided not to continue this independent campaign to run for president. Let them know that we can make a bigger impact with U.S.ofA., our new eco-friendly marketing-slash-employment service for products and services that help sustain our planet's resources."

After Gray typed in his father's words on his laptop, he stared at the words on the screen and nodded as if pleased with what he saw. Then Gray clicked his mouse a few times and brought up on his screen the cartoon-like image of himself riding on the back of the green snail that represented his father. He pointed to the government buildings in the distance and said, "We're American slugs moving our government in a direction that creates jobs promoting products and services that sustain our planet. So we work to improve the planet first. The politicians will only stop resisting change when slugs *are* the politicians."

"Exactly!" Danny agreed, adding, "Even though slugs are the majority now ... they are not organized with leaders who represent them!"

"Right!"

On their way back to their office, Gray said something that gave his dad the best news he'd heard since Gray told him he wanted to move to Omaha. "Since we're starting U.S.ofA. together, I feel more involved and I really want to see just where we can take this ... together."

Danny only smiled and told his son that they had better get to work.

I Saw My Father's Fear

THAT FIRST WEEKEND after letting their "constituents" know that there would be no slide toward the White House, Gray went for a late-night walk alone down by the riverfront. He had been thinking about two separate, unrelated moments in his life. Each of these moments he was certain had to be related to the self-confidence any man of any age must have—especially two men involved in a race for the highest office in the land. Both of these moments met in Gray's mind and held his attention along the bike path near the river. Combined together, they helped his confused mind reach a place of understanding about his dad's abrupt decision to cancel his political aspirations to run as an independent slug for president.

One of the moments happened when his dad wasn't even around. Gray was seated in the school auditorium after he had been living with his father in Omaha for just a couple of months. He didn't have any friends yet, and that was okay with him. It was a Friday afternoon homecoming pep rally for the football game to be played later that night. Gray hated football; he always compared it to America's way of preparing for war. A "foreign" team invades the "home" team's turf, forcing the home team to defend its ground. The masses rally and cry for their brave warriors to keep attacking the enemy and defending their ground, while the women cheer them on to victory.

Seated a couple rows in front of Gray and a few seats to his right was the most beautiful girl in the whole school. She was a perfect symbol to all those brave young men who give their all in battle. Every senior boy knew that the beautiful Cray Lane was out of everyone's league because they all knew that she only dated college guys from Lincoln. And most were jocks with money.

When the obnoxious pep rally was over and the student body got to their feet to leave the auditorium—all happy to get out of school a little early—that was the moment beautiful Cray turned back and looked right at him. There was no doubt about it; she had smiled at him as if she knew him and really liked him. Even other guys near turned his way to see who Cray was smiling at. *But I was a coward,* he recalled telling himself all the way home from school and the rest of that weekend.

He had seen her plainly holding back her steps to leave

the auditorium, a purposeful and bold way to show him that she would like to meet him in the aisle, to walk away together on their way to freedom. She was so used to having older guys with more confidence approach her and talk to her. Seeing this new boy's fear of an encounter with her only confirmed why she preferred older boys or jocks. They had been brave in battles and didn't see physical beauty as something to fear.

Loping along the lit trail, Gray could hear the river rushing south off to his right. His neck was warmed by his anger upon recalling his cowardly inaction. His wall of fear kept him far enough away from an image named Cray, that nice girl who only wanted to flirt and interact for a brief moment. It was a harmless encounter that he wished he had realized at the time was just that. Instead, as he climbed the steps with her well ahead of his cowardly pace, it made him recall another moment many years ago when he was with his father in a restaurant in San Diego.

This is how my dad must've felt, he remembered telling his mind during that walk down those auditorium steps, feeling the shame of a coward with every single step.

It had been one of those perfect San Diego summer mornings when he was just a boy. His father had just picked him up at his mother's house, and they were off in his rental car to begin one of their glorious summer vacations. Just the two of them. They stopped to have breakfast at a place his dad always liked to go to before they hit the road. Their waitress was a sweet young woman who seemed to young Gray to be flirting with his dad. He asked his dad if he liked their waitress.

"Nice waitresses get better tips," Danny winked at his

young son.

When they were leaving the restaurant, they literally ran into an ugly scene going on near the back door of the restaurant where their rental car was parked. A large, muscular, nicely dressed older man had their waitress forcefully pressed against the back door. He had to be her father. He was screaming into her face about the way she was living her life. Both Danny and Gray couldn't move a muscle or even say anything. That's when Gray saw his father's fear of getting involved, of stepping into a situation that was trouble. The man had grabbed her forearms that she held up to protect her face as his angry words combined with her plaintive pleadings to stop.

Gray kept looking up at his dad to do something, to help this nice girl with such a sweet personality who had just served them breakfast. As they got into their rental car while this angry father was manhandling his daughter, Gray recalled his dad saying, "It's none of our business."

In the Omaha night on his walk back home, Gray was pondering his dad's confusion weeks ago. His dad was talking about being the Commander-in-Chief and how he was not the type of man who could be responsible for sending American troops into harm's way. Gray recalled how brave his dad was with Darin Bain, going into that house in harm's way. But then it came to Gray that his dad felt responsible for Renee being in a hostage situation, and that's why he took action.

Back and forth he went, seeing again that fear on his father's face and the terrified resignation outside that restaurant. It was as if the man of today had to prove to the man back then that he could be calm and brave and take action in a storm of potential violence, as he had in Council Bluffs

And yes, he's right, Gray admitted to himself, *My dad is no Commander-in-Chief ... and never could be.*

Yet in some distant election, Gray was certain that a man like his father would be needed to unite the nation's growing number of slugs who have consciously decided it's time to stop the insanity of defense spending and begin to put a priority on uniting our energies to consciously maintain the resources we all need and take from the earth and seas.

Yes, Dad, you have given me the best work I can imagine. When you left me in San Diego, you said you were coming back for me and that you were working hard for both of us so that we could live well when we were together. You have done that, Dad. Thank you.

Garden of Slugs

B Y THE BEGINNING of 2015, even the Telemaster chiropractic clients now knew the company as U.S.ofA., a marketing and employment service with over two million members receiving its newsletter and accessing its website. Big changes came from focused action directed by Danny and Gray, a team that had taken a very successful service for chiropractors and turned it into a one-of-a-kind employment agency and marketing service for eco-friendly products and services. Their service was so successful and well-received that they had opened a new branch every thirty days since May 2014. These U.S.ofA. branches started out in eight small cities in eight of the most populous states in the country. Each manager of these branches was an original Omaha Telemaster slug who was willing to relocate to the new satellite location that Danny selected personally. Each branch was opened in an area with a green-minded workforce of slugs who were already subscribers of U.S.ofA.'s *Peaceful Trails* newsletter.

Danny's experienced slugs at the Slug Central location in Omaha were now marketing an array of solar and wind products, along with carbon-free vehicles and machinery to business prospects interested in a green and sustainable America. U.S.ofA. was marketing numerous organic food products that small businesses wanted to expand to retail businesses. These were all products and services thoroughly researched by Danny's slugs in Omaha. Darin Bain, the onetime "hostage-taker of Council Bluffs," was put in charge of researching and test-marketing a homeopathic mind stabilizer for slugs diagnosed as bipolar. Putting himself on this product, right away he noticed a dramatic overall improvement in his mood swings after getting off his medication. The new herbal supplement would be sold exclusively to health food stores.

Eventually, Bain became the production manager of this new product line, which turned into twice the income and hours for him that he had been getting. In the fall of 2014, he was able to move out of the Butter Roast studio and into a nicer place. A short time later, the manufacturer of the bipolar product U.S.ofA. slugs were marketing wanted Darin Bain to move to their home office and work for them for three times the salary. When his boss heard the news, Danny shook the hand of his happy slug who had turned his life around and said with a huge grin on his face, "Bye, Darin."

It was an incredible time to be one of Danny's slugs in Omaha—to be a part of a united, synergistic team that was finding new clients and conscious consumers who believed in sustaining the planet's limited resources. "Insatiable is Not Sustainable" replaced the mantra "Slow down ... there's plenty of time" that revolved around Slug Central.

U.S.ofA.'s growth was moving Gray and Danny to higher levels of creativity. The boss had seen early on that expanding his new version of Telemaster demanded that his theory "love is money" be practiced before withholding and waiting prevailed. Instead of setting up a 401(k) plan for his slugs—a financial instrument that would always be run by Wall Street and the public's level of confidence in the economy—the King of Slugs paid his slugs a much higher hourly wage. He proved he was not going to withhold money from them while he prospered. The more money he paid his slugs, the more his slugs animated with confidence and contagious enthusiasm. Consequently, more quality appointments, leads, and sales were made.

There was still zero competition among U.S.ofA. slugs with no posted stats or bonuses for only the top producers. Now more than ever there was a united wave of energy that Danny had never seen in all his days in telemarketing.

One U.S.ofA. client—Greenhouse Nursery located in Woodbury, Iowa—had been contacted by one of Danny's slugs to market their trees and plants to commercial prospects in the nearby bigger cities of Des Moines, Sioux Falls, and Omaha. Free delivery with a minimum order was offered to prospective clients, and an incredible website was designed by Gray. Soon U.S.ofA. went to work finding quality prospects interested in having a Greenhouse rep contact them about their products. As a result, their business boomed to the degree that their happy client had to buy two new trucks for deliveries.

Because of the Greenhouse Nursery success, whenever one of their trucks was making deliveries in Omaha the driver was routed to drop off a few free plants and trees to U.S.ofA. Within a few short months, Slug Central was turned into a "Garden of Slugs," as Danny called it, which increased the air quality and positive atmosphere markedly. And with the Greenhouse Nursery success, U.S.ofA. in Omaha was able to find other nursery clients in every new satellite location, literally planting office spaces in green and naturally creating new work for dozens of slugs related to the wholesale nursery and garden industry.

Happy chiropractic clients that Omaha slugs had been calling for were handed over to new satellite locations so that Omaha slugs could find and secure new clients. Like chiropractic and nursery clients, every new "green" client would be duplicated after Omaha slugs proved it was a marketable and viable eco-friendly product or service. Companies like Amanda's Organic Dog and Cat Food, a small business that was contacted by Omaha slugs, were catapulted into marketplace success. Within six short months of signing with U.S.ofA., Amanda's was employing three hundred new slugs and shipping their product to new retailers all over the country.

After a year, U.S.ofA. slugs were increasing markedly

because of the growing number of U.S.ofA. satellites and Gray's constant attention to their website.

Hundreds of large corporations, including some with green products and services, contacted U.S.ofA. wanting to advertise on their website. Always Danny gave them the same response: "Ads are a nuisance to our slugs. They voted on it and told me so."

*   *   *

By the end of 2015, there were twenty-three U.S.ofA. satellite locations in twenty-three states employing over seven hundred slugs. From Gray's stats he reported that the total new slugs hired by U.S.ofA. clients because of those seven hundred slugs totaled a little over five thousand. That meant that each U.S.ofA. slug had created Earth-friendly employment for about seven slugs. Danny was elated with that seven-to-one ratio because the old Telemaster alone had generated not quite one new slug per chiropractor. After these numbers were confirmed by Gray, Danny told his son, "We're onto something, here."

The pay for managers was an important part in keeping each new location running smoothly. A manager would make twice the $15.00 per hour rate of his slugs. This was generous and fair because managers worked both shifts and worked a minimum of forty-five hours a week with no overtime. Twelve hundred a week to work in a cooperative, stress-reduced environment did not create what Danny called "trickle-down resentment" that CEOs and executives in big corporations naturally cause because of their ridiculously high salaries and bonuses that are driven by greed for higher profits for shareholders. It was the manager's job to replicate and maintain the team-like harmony of U.S.ofA. in Omaha. Gray set up a Slug Skype at each new location. That way Danny could see and hear for himself what was going on at each location.

Yes, U.S.ofA. had a king, someone who set the pace and made the important decisions that kept each location a productive and positive environment for his slugs. As always, the real work started with Danny's slugs. If they were happy, they would provide work for their clients by finding them customers who believed in doing something positive for the planet.

U.S.ofA. was truly growing into a garden of slugs, furnished with plants and purified air products, ergonomic office furniture, and healthcare plans for non-smokers after ninety days. Each cube had a purified water dispenser that was furnished by another happy client. Danny Mack truly cared about all his employees, showing them that they had the power to build the kind of America they wanted.

Trail of Hope

G RAY WAS STARTING to have second thoughts about his father's decision to not run for any political office, especially after U.S.ofA. *Peaceful Trails* subscribers had reached four million readers by early 2016. One weekend night in March 2016 Gray told Danny, "You know, slugs can at least determine the outcome of who will become the next president … even if you don't run, Dad."

"I can't tell them who to vote for. Even if I ran as an independent, they can vote for anybody they want. You know that."

"All I know, Dad, is you gave so many slugs hope that someone could really go for it all and then reach it. Now you could run and just talk about your success with U.S.ofA. and how you can unite the whole country. Big business won't support you, but most slugs will. We now have millions of members who will get you on the ballot in every state."

"What's the average age of our members now?" Danny asked.

"Twenty-four."

"Why don't you run?"

"Me? For president?"

"Yeah. You'll be twenty-two this summer."

"I'm too young to be the president."

"You're the one who puts together the website. Over ninety percent of our slugs who work for U.S.ofA. found us because of your creative employment ads. And just last month, what was the most popular campaign proposal that you said the next president should make?"

"That defense spending should be cut in half, and the money saved should be spent on the country's infrastructure," Gray said.

"Exactly. Roads, bridges ... plenty of construction work for unemployed slugs willing to work. Your generation needs and wants leaders *now* who have to get this country united and moving ahead for all working slugs, not just Wall Street."

"But you're the King of Slugs, Dad ... not me."

"When I retire or die, you will be. *If* that's what you want. Right now I like the idea of supporting independent slugs who run for Congress, the House or Senate ... so they can change and create laws."

"We can do that by using our website to let members know which independent politicians need their support. Over four million slugs gives us some leverage to support new independent slugs running for any office."

Danny agreed.

"Ya know, Dad, supporting independents who run for Congress doesn't seem so daunting or ..."

"Impossible?"

"Right!"

* * *

Every day and night of 2016 was all about politics in America. Once again, there was no viable candidate running as an independent for president.

U.S.ofA. continued growing like gangbusters as an eco-friendly job creator. When magazines pursued the King of Slugs to be on their cover to promote him as the next Steve Jobs, Danny refused. He told them each in matter-of-fact terms that he was not at all interested in promoting a corporate media publication that encouraged unconscious consumerism.

U.S.ofA. *Peaceful Trails* subscribership also grew despite the end of Danny's trail of hope, a campaign slide to the White House. Gray felt better about sliding away from politics after doing some extensive research on presidential voting projections for the fall. The numbers revealed clearly that they would not slide past either of the two parties, let alone both of them. His projection was that not until 2024 would it be mathematically feasible for any independent politician to have a real shot at winning a considerable number of elected seats in the House and Senate, let alone the biggest seat of all in the Oval Office. And by 2024 his dad would be in his sixties, too old to represent the thirty-four-year-old average age of slugs who were paying the entitlements promised to their parents and baby boomer grandparents.

"Maybe you'll run in 2032 and be the youngest president ever," Danny remarked to his son one night. "How many members are we projected to have in 2032?"

"About thirty-six million."

"Wow! Not bad, huh?" he smiled at his son from his recliner.

Gray went to bed that night after finishing reading one of his dad's books that he'd given him way back when his dad took him back to San Diego after one of their summer vacations. The book was an old paperback biography on the rock star Jim Morrison of The Doors. Written in 1979, Danny was about Gray's age now when he first read the book in the early '80s. As Gray listened to the wind flapping the row of flags outside his bedroom window, he recalled Jim Morrison's comment about how American boys are the only people who can dream of becoming president. Coming from Morrison it sounded like a self-centered, ego-driven desire that was unique to American boys—as if they have a God complex that tells them they can be president someday.

Gray turned on his side to face the lit dial of his alarm clock and realized he was one of those American boys Morrison was talking about. Gray knew he was the son of a popular man—a man famous in his field—and that because of his father he could get millions of votes *if* he wanted that kind of life and that kind of reality that would fill his ego to the very brim. Then he thought of U.S.ofA. and the growing numbers of people who were working hard as United Slugs of America, making a real difference in a world that is destined to explode in population in just a few decades. *All these drastic weather changes causing droughts and famines ... and the changes that have to be made by men and women who declare war on wars and spend those wasted trillions for war instead on learning how to live well together on one united planet ... when no religions or countries teach their young that it's noble and good to die for a good cause.* Gray could see his father soaring high, being one of those new leaders in business without the resistance that running for president would bring. *And I could be with him, creating more jobs for slugs while new independent slugs who want to be the future politicians can get the support that they will need to get elected. Yes! That will be the new world ... someday.*

Gray nodded off to sleep.

That same night, Danny stopped for a moment to stand outside his son's bedroom door. He was a grateful father who could be thankful for the boy who motivated him to find a better way of life. He, too, wanted to become president when he was Gray's age. And he had come closer than most men. But now he, like his son, knew they had something better than the White House; they had U.S.ofA. and real hope for a united America.

Crazy Together

I T WAS IN 2020 that U.S.ofA. took it upon itself to move the U.S. Postal Service toward showing a profit, making good on one of Danny's earlier campaign proposals. Danny Mack contracted with the government to telemarket his idea to small businesses all over the country of selling personalized "Slug Stamps" to small business owners. Businesses willing to buy a minimum of ten thousand Slug Stamps at a buck a stamp could advertise their businesses. This was Danny's way to move America's sluggish Postal Service out of the red.

The response was incredible. U.S.ofA. generated enough prepaid orders for Slug Stamps that the Postal Service showed a giant profit after the first two years. It also solved their growing pension issues without forced retirements for postal workers who wanted to continue working.

In 2023 Danny submitted a proposal to Congress to have Slug Stamps marketed by U.S.ofA. to individual consumers as well as small businesses. The profits would be used exclusively toward reducing the nation's thirty-trillion-dollar debt, so that the country's crumbling infrastructure could be addressed. Congress voted it down in a close vote. In the proposal, big corporations with off-shore tax shelters were not allowed to buy Slug Stamps because they were not paying their fair share of taxes that regular slugs had to pay. When Congress rejected Danny's proposal because of backroom politics, that's when Gray Mack decided to run for the nation's highest office.

It took Danny and Gray eight more years—until 2031—to get U.S.ofA. on the ballot in all fifty states as an independent party. With America forty trillion dollars in debt and baby boomers living longer than any previous generation of Americans, there was only one bright spot in the country: the Postal Service had shown an ever-increasing profit since 2024 when the King of Slugs was appointed Postmaster General by President Ruben Martinez.

Two months before what proved to be a close election, Danny and Gray met with Mr. Martinez, who offered to appoint Danny as Postmaster General if the King of Slugs endorsed him in the upcoming election.

Danny and his son took a whole week to come up with a proposal for Mr. Martinez, knowing that if he was elected there would be far less resistance in America to forming an independent political party such as U.S.ofA. In one referendum poll by U.S.ofA., eighty percent of Hispanic U.S.ofA. members responded that they would vote for a U.S.ofA. candidate instead of a Hispanic candidate who was a Democrat or Republican.

When Mr. Martinez convened with Danny and Gray in Omaha at Slug Central, the Hispanic candidate agreed to appoint Danny Mack as Postmaster General whether or not he endorsed him for president. The King of Slugs said he would only accept the appointment if he could run the Postal Service like he ran his business in Omaha. And Danny's terms were blunt: No more random junk mail; machinery that eliminated jobs and damaged packages would be replaced by slugs in need of a job; and Slug Stamps could be marketed to individuals wanting their face or business on a stamp, with profits applied to the nation's debt.

Martinez accepted the terms, and one of the first things he did when elected was appoint Danny as Postmaster General. Within three days Danny replaced every supervisor in the Postal Service with U.S.ofA. members. Supervisors who didn't want to retire had to go off the clock into their nearest postal distribution center where they would find and return to the senders every lost or damaged piece of mail that wasn't auctioned off and put toward the nation's debt. Needless to say, there were union protests and suits filed by about 3,500 postal supervisors who either quit or were dismissed for incompetence.

The King of Slugs' guarantee to the American people was also blunt: "The U.S. Postal Service will show a profit every quarter, even if I have to fire every slug that works there and replace them with one of my slugs."

In his first ninety days at the helm of the Postal Service, many veteran slugs were terminated and forced to retire early because of poor attitude and incompetence. Danny Mack soon had thousands of enemies who didn't care about the dramatic turnaround the Postal Service was making. But the rest of the country loved their new Postmaster General who meditated and used an inversion table in his office every morning. He was an incredible leader who brought efficiency into another "slug central." He eliminated petty penny increases in postage rates by freezing the price of a first-class letter at fifty cents and prioritizing all mail with zero tolerance for any lost or damaged mail.

In less than twenty-four months, Danny had the Postal Service not only showing a profit but actually paying off a big chunk of the national debt's annual interest.

In 2026 Danny told his son, referring to the Postal Service success, "This is our way onto the ballot in '32 ... if you want it."

It took the U.S.ofA. five more years to get on the ballot in all fifty states as an independent party.

*   *   *

August 8th, 2032, U.S.ofA. had its first convention to announce its nominee for president in the Omaha Convention Center, a media-hyped venue that was sold out six months before the convention. The building was filled to the rafters with over eighteen thousand registered independent voters, most of them U.S.ofA. members from all over the country. It was the night Gray Mack was to accept his party's nomination and announce his running mate for the election in early November.

All fifty states had delegates from U.S.ofA., with an estimated thirty-eight million members registered and ready to vote for Gray and his soon-to-be-announced running mate. The media found out that if you ask anyone inside the convention center who Gray Mack wanted on his party ticket, they all had the same answer: The former Postmaster General who resigned earlier in the summer—the King of Slugs.

Backstage, a dressing room was guarded by Secret Service agents where Burt and Shelly sat across from Danny and Gray. Burt looked at his watch and told them they had ten minutes before their campaign song would begin.

"That's when we go?" Gray asked.

Burt nodded yes.

Gray asked Burt and Shelly. "Would you mind excusing yourselves so I can have a few words with Dad?"

Alone in the dressing room, it occurred to Gray that both he and his father were too casually dressed for such an important event. They were dressed as if they were going on summer vacation together. When Gray started to talk, his words were spoken as if in a dream—aloof and far away. "This has been our 'crazy together' thing we always talked about doing, Dad."

His father could only nod as a distant rap on the dressing room door told them it was time to head for the stage.

In an instant they were approaching one of the wings

backstage and could now hear the campaign song "Veracruz" as Burt and Shelly trailed them. That's when Gray stopped walking with his father to listen to the music and see on a nearby TV monitor the crowd waiting for them. It was the first time the media was able to show these two independent slugs who refused to be interviewed or participate in any debates covered by the mainstream media.

Now the rest of the world could see the convention center filled with United Slugs of America, each of them somebody living under great stress and each one in attendance to support the father-and-son independent ticket that was unique to American politics. Viewers could see this was truly a different kind of convention with the crowd subdued, swaying back and forth to the haunting sound of "Veracruz," a song they had heard a thousand times while at work. There was no us-versus-them energy here. It was eighteen thousand Americans holding hands and swaying back and forth to the music while on their feet, all the while conscious that they had worked together because of this father-and-son team who wanted to do something crazy together. It was a united gathering of working people who knew they did good work together.

Backstage a host of security couldn't prevent the shot that came from behind a velvet curtain—a popping sound that sounded like a firecracker. It was Danny who was hit and fell over onto Gray as Shelly screamed and Secret Service agents swarmed all over a man with a handgun dressed in a postal uniform. Gray could see that the gunman resembled Darin Bain when he had taken his ex-wife hostage.

Gray cradled his father in his arms and Danny's relaxed face whispered to his son, "We can edit this out." Then the King of Slugs was gone.

Gray bolted up in bed, thankful it was only a dream. As he heard the familiar flapping sound of so many flags waving in the wind outside his bedroom window, he was absolutely clear from that moment on that he wanted no part of some angry coward with a gun to diminish all the crazy-together good work he and his father were doing with thousands of slugs all over America.

The End

"Writing a novel is
like leaving a safe
and worn path
in order to take a
route nobody has
ever taken. It's
dangerous and
risky, and all for
the hope of finding
you, my reader."

www.michaelfrederick82.com

WGRL-HQ FIC
31057101488768
FIC FREDE
Frederick, Michael.
King of slugs : a novel

12/13